THE SOULMATE JUNKIE

AND OTHER STORIES OF FANTASY AND SCIENCE FICTION

DAVID H. HENDRICKSON

Penucket Publishing

It's love at first sight.

Or at least heart-pounding, wing-flapping, propagate-the-species-and-I-mean-now-baby-now animal lust. Insect lust, which even the dumbest primate knows is the best kind, the reason we're going to swarm over the entire world some day. Cover every last inch with our hard exoskeletons, our three pairs of legs, and our clicking mandibles. More specifically, I'm feeling praying mantis lust, the most supreme and powerful of all lusts.

Green means go, baby.

PRAISE FOR DAVID H. HENDRICKSON

"A fantastic writer, one of our best working right now." - Dean Wesley Smith, *USA Today* bestselling writer

"David H. Hendrickson is one of my favorite writers."- Kristine Kathryn Rusch, *USA Today* bestselling writer

ISBN-13: 978-1-948134-20-0

CONTENTS

INTRODUCTION

spent countless hours and a bajillion words on previous drafts of this introduction, vainly trying to say something intelligent and insightful about these stories. Those drafts all ended where they belonged. In my electronic wastebasket.

Hey, maybe "intelligent and insightful" just ain't my shtick. Or perhaps these stories defy coherent comments. (I humbly offer for your consideration before you even read it, "The Birth of Booger Nation." Take a wild guess, sight unseen, as to how consistently it fits under any possible umbrella comments about the rest of these stories. I rest my case.)

Maybe it all just comes down to this. I'm an entertainer. For your hard-earned (unless, of course, you stole it) money, I hope to provide you with a good time. Stories of the imagination expand the worlds a writer can explore. And given that freedom to explore, the writer of such stories can offer more opportunities for a good time than, for example, yet another dreary literary novel about a college professor going through a mid-life crisis and sleeping with a student.

These stories of the imagination are the best ones I have to offer, the best I haven't previously collected or reserved for my upcoming collection that merges crime and fantasy, *Crime Fantastique: Stories of Mystery and Suspense*.

I hope you love them all. Yes, even "The Birth of Booger Nation." *Especially* "The Birth of Booger Nation."

THE SOULMATE JUNKIE AND
THE BEATING HEART

INTRODUCTION TO THE
SOULMATE JUNKIE AND THE
BEATING HEART

I wrote this story for an anthology themed on factories. *Factories?* What on Earth was I going to write about to fit *that* theme? (Well, duh, I guess I was going to write about factories, but... what the heck was I going to write about?) At first, I was stumped. But who doesn't like a challenge? Besides, this anthology would be edited by Ron and Brigid Collins, both terrific writers, editors, and friends.

I could envision possible science fiction stories centered around glistening, futuristic factories in outer space. Earth-bound factories, by contrast, conjured up for me, a lifelong New England resident, nothing but gritty old brick buildings in various states of disrepair, typically in dying old mill towns along the likes of the Merrimack River.

Depressing. Who would want to read about that? And on a purely selfish note, who would want to write about that? Not me.

At the same time, outer space ain't exactly my shtick. I've written a few such stories, had a great time doing it, and been delighted with the results. But that's far from my wheelhouse and even more importantly, if that's the "low-hanging fruit" to which other writers might flock, I would want to zig while they zagged.

Somewhere along the way, the concept of a soulmate junkie popped into my creative subconscious, and I was off and running. I was delighted with the result—the quintessential story that never would have gotten written if not for an editor's anthology call—but as with many, if not most, stories, you never really know until an editor gives the thumbs up.

Ron and Brigid loved "Soulmate Junkie," and it was destined to appear in *Factory Effect*. Until, that is, the pandemic hit and forced the cancellation of the book. I felt bad for Ron and Brigid, who had invested so much time and energy into the project, as well as the other writers, but there was a happy ending for this story.

Dean Wesley Smith scooped it up for *Pulphouse Fiction Magazine*, where it led off the October 2021 issue. In his introduction, he even called it "maybe one of the most powerful SF stories I have read in some time."

THE SOULMATE JUNKIE AND THE BEATING HEART

*E*mily Jones, her shoulders slumped and eyes bloodshot, swiped her badge at the entrance of the crumbling, three-story, red brick building. Located on the banks of the Merrimack River in an impoverished, old mill town north of Boston, the building stood as tall as it was wide and deep, a hundred fifty feet of grime in each direction. A black smokestack on the far left near the back fouled the air with a dank, musky odor.

Outside, no sign announced the business's name, though cars filled the side parking lot. Inside the windowless, antiseptic foyer that ran the full width of the building but extended only fifteen feet deep, a sign in old English script with exaggerated curlicues read, *La fabrique d'amour.*

The Love Factory.

As if spelling it out in French made what Emily and all the others did in this dungeon suddenly romantic and exciting. A sour taste filled Emily's mouth. She swiped her credit card-sized badge across the scanner beside the middle of five heavy metal doors, and after the beep, pulled it open. As she walked past the side stairwell and its surveillance camera, then down the cavernous, concrete-walled corridor, the door clanged shut behind her, sounding like the closing of a door to a prison cell.

Another day of her sentence.

Twenty-nine years old, she felt like seventy-nine. No beauty, but not physically repulsive either, Emily had limp, shoulder-length, auburn hair, a pug nose that she knew cried out for cosmetic surgery, a flat chest that cried out even more, and an extra twenty-five pounds she'd been trying unsuccessfully to rid herself of for all her adult life. Most noticeable of all, though, she looked worn out and used up, her brown eyes vacant and downcast, her lips grim and never smiling.

No wonder Mark was thinking of leaving her. Probably more than just thinking, too. It had to be a lead-pipe certainty.

But he was supposed to be *the one*. They were supposed to be *soulmates*. Like John and Kevin and Jason and Tom and Jared and Ryan before Mark. Now, like all those before him, Mark was growing distant. Cold.

Even though she'd crossed the line she swore she'd never cross. Emily had become not just an employee, but a customer.

Her footfalls echoed down the corridor, as did those of five or six other faceless employees, until she stopped in front of the door to unit 349A. She swiped her badge across yet another scanner and stepped inside what she'd come to think of as her tomb. It was a thin sliver of a room, the air heavy and humid. More closet than room, really. Though barely more than five feet tall, Emily could hold out her arms and simultaneously touch both side walls. The far wall stood less than ten feet from the door. The ceiling only seven feet high. Its barren walls painted industrial green, "the tomb" smelled faintly of mildew and Lysol at the same.

It held only one thing: the chamber. When she had first come to work there, she had thought it looked like a tanning bed. Slide in and pull down the lid, though she did so fully clothed. Now, though, she thought of it as a coffin.

Emily slid into the chamber, pushed her badge into the slot in the lid above her, and pulled the lid down. Her balance glowed on the screen above her.

0.00

And that was after the emergency withdrawal from her bank account to rectify yesterday's negative balance after too many purchases of the company's products. A bank account that was now as dry and empty as she was, with no more funds to cover any emergency, no matter how dire.

Even if it was the difference between Mark leaving her or not.

So it was time to get to work. Again. Too many hours because of too many purchases. Emily's fingers itched and her mouth felt dry. Deep inside her chest, her heart ached. She wanted to cry even though it wasn't yet time for that.

Swallowing hard, Emily touched her fingertips to the recessed sensors on both sides of her. She began to read from the built-in screen on the lid. In no time, her fingertips tingled, and the air smelled of ozone. Tears streamed down the sides of her face, blurring the words on the screen until she blinked the tears away. Emily devoured the words and emitted her premium-cut emotions into the fingertip sensors.

She began to cry. Her sobs grew louder and more forceful until her entire body shook, wracked with their pain. Even so, she held her fingertips to the sensors, never losing contact.

The consummate professional.

At the beginning, it had been her dream job. Get paid to read romance novels. She already did that for free! What was the catch? Compared to her previous position as a social worker—having her heart ripped out on a daily basis and then having to come back the next day to do it all over again—the position of Senior Emotopath felt like stealing the company's money.

It was *so* easy. Like the proverbial taking candy from babies. During her job interview she scored highly—off the charts, actually—in the company's "emotion emission" scores.

Emily *oozed* emotion. It poured out of her like sweat from a fat man in a sauna. She was hired on the spot as a Senior Emotopath. No junior designation. No probationary period. No references. Can you start now?

"Today?" she had asked.

"Now!"

She needed no mentor or training. Emily was a natural.

She hit all her quotas and then kept going, accumulating bonus after bonus. The company drew off her "premium-level" emotion emissions, distilled and matured them in the emoto-vats that filled the entire basement floor below, then added them to its products. Emily's exported emotions, as well as those of the other Emotopaths, were the key ingredient in the company's Soulmates Series of couple's jewelry, guaranteed to draw both partners closer together than ever—make them true soulmates, the one and only for each other—as well as the potent essence in the Soulmates perfume and cologne lines, designed to attract a soulmate to the lonely wearer of the scent.

According to the company-sponsored research, the products worked.. They were no late-night infomercial gimmicks. There was no placebo effect. *They worked!*

Not all the time, of course. There had to be *some* element of destiny involved. Otherwise, what was the point? One couldn't *totally* manufacture the pure joy of being soulmates. No Emotopath emissions—even Emily's supercharged ones, no matter how distilled and matured—could turn Joan of Arc and Attila the Hun into soulmates.

You couldn't just bathe in Soulmates bubble bath or splash on Soulmates perfume or cologne and then automatically ensnare the object of your desire. Gotcha! Never going to let you go.

There was always free will and the element of chance. But the jewelry, perfumes, colognes, and the rest of the product line could help when that little something extra was needed.

Like with Mark.

And so Emily had bought them matching Soulmates watchbands. And they had become immediately closer. More intimate in every way.

When that began to wear off, she'd bought them the special couple's version of Soulmates perfume and cologne, designed not to attract someone new but to maintain and strengthen a pre-existing bond.

And that at least *seemed* to work. For a while.

But when even that effect flickered, when she'd eventually gone through the entire company catalog, working countless overtime hours to pay for it all, she resorted to a secret benefit available only to employees, though not one that would ever appear in a corporate Human Resources handbook.

Who, Emily asked herself, could ever put a price on true love?

After pouring all of her emotions into the fingertip sensors, she checked on her balance, entered the secret code, and withdrew the entire balance on as much of the pure stuff as her money could buy.

The purest of the pure. Uncut. As far from the watered down, commercially available Soulmate products as the purest heroin in Afghanistan was to the stomped-on, diluted imitator being sold four blocks away from the factory.

Emily let it pour over her. It would make her irresistibly attractive to Mark, bind them together like never before. Forever and ever.

Soulmates at last.

She could feel his presence atop her in the chamber. He wasn't actually there, of course; there wasn't enough room for a couple inside the chamber no matter how petite they might both be, and Mark was almost six feet tall and two hundred pounds.

But she felt his presence nonetheless. Smelled the spicy cinnamon fragrance of his Soulmates cologne. Tasted the minty taste of Soulmates mouthwash on his lips. Felt his facial hair brush pleasantly against her cheeks.

In her mind, Emily wrapped her arms around him.

Held him close. Closer. And closer still. She felt his weight pressing upon her in the most pleasurable of places.

They were meant for each other. Nothing could tear them asunder.

Soulmates forever.

EMILY HAD NEVER BEFORE TESTED the limits of her badge's access, but she was desperate now. Beyond desperate.

When she had returned to the small, studio apartment she and Mark shared following her immersion in the Soulmate purest of the pure, she had wrapped her arms around him every bit as tightly as she had imagined in the chamber and they had made love feverishly for their longest time ever. They hadn't just rutted like animals. They had...

Made.

Love.

Like only true soulmates could do.

And then they had enjoyed a wonderful dinner of coconut shrimp, chicken-stuffed crepes, and brownies a la mode. They went for a long walk, hand in hand, her head resting on his shoulder. And come back to the apartment and made wonderful, soulmate love all over again.

Just the way Emily had envisioned they would spend the rest of their lives.

But lying together in bed this morning, Mark had turned his face away when she went to kiss him—"For the love of God, could you brush your teeth first?" he'd begged

—and then added, "And while you're at it, could you take a shower?"

As if his own breath didn't stink, and the dried-sweat remnants of their lovemaking weren't on him, too. Hell, his hair was sticking up every which way like a goddamn doofus. *Your shit stinks, too, buddy.*

But it wasn't the smell of his breath or their mutually dried, stale sweat that bothered Emily. It was that *it mattered*.

"For the love of God, could you brush your teeth first?" and, "while you're at it, could you take a shower?" were not the pillow talk of soulmates.

What Emily knew she needed was a more potent or a longer-lasting, perhaps infinite supply of the pure stuff that had made last night so magical. Even if her bank account was empty and her work balance not a penny over 0.00.

She'd worked *so* many hours lately to pay for everything. She felt so drained of energy, particularly emoto-energy, she doubted she could conjure up much of a balance lying there in her chamber. And whatever balance she could manage, it would be only the smallest fraction of what she needed right now. Needed to restore last night's bliss of her relationship with Mark.

And dammit, didn't she *deserve* it? Not just the result—the bliss of a soulmate relationship—but the product, too. Didn't she deserve the purest of the pure, uncut emoto-essence. Should she really have had to pay so dearly the day before? Wasn't her essence the most premium of them all? She had no idea how the company distilled and matured it, transforming her raw essence into a finished product, but they were gouging her just to get back a piece of herself!

It wasn't fair.

If she didn't have the funds to buy back her own essence in distilled and finished form—and she most certainly didn't—then maybe she should just *take it*. Take back what was hers to begin with! Or maybe she could even form an alliance with others who needed the primo product as much as she did? Convince the company to do right by them and give them back a piece of themselves for free.

Emily thought of the drawn faces and haggard looks of her fellow Emotopaths, most of them women but a few of them men, always looking down as they walked to their chambers, never wasting an emotion on a co-worker, on a fellow traveler on this road to nowhere. Were all of them as dependent—as desperate for love eternal in the form of soulmates—as she was?

Not that she was actually desperate, of course. Emily thought, though, that the rest of them probably were. But would they be of any help in getting what they so dearly required? Or would they just get in the way?

Or would there not be enough to go around? Might she have to share a little too much and not be left enough to give her and Mark their happily ever after?

Emily decided to go it alone.

IT TOOK three skin-crawling days before Emily got her chance. A red-headed woman she did not recognize, bright-eyed and bushy-tailed with broad shoulders, muscular arms —a new hire?—was entering the building at the same time as Emily. Big Red, as Emily instantly nicknamed her, swiped her badge to enter the stairwell and headed down the circular stairs. Emily caught the door just before it closed and ducked inside. Company policy, of course, strictly forbade tailgating, but Emily figured company policy also forbade employees stealing back what was rightfully theirs.

She followed Big Red down the winding metal steps, their footfalls echoing in the claustrophobic air until they reached the heavy metal door to the basement floor. Big Red swiped her badge against the sensor, and stepped inside.

Emily followed.

Big Red frowned. "You work here?"

Emily nodded. "Transferred."

Big Red nodded, then headed down the long corridor with Emily in her wake. The corridor was as cavernous as the one upstairs, but it looked like there were only doors on the right side.

"Where you headed?" Big Red asked.

That was the million dollar question, wasn't it? Emily mustered as nonchalant and confident of a look as she could manage and said, "Emoto-vat."

Big Red nodded, but then gave a quizzical look. "We went past the door." She pointed to the lone door on the left twenty-feet behind them. Not knowing it was there, Emily had missed it.

"Yeah, right," Emily said, then headed back to the vat door. She felt Big Red's eyes on her back, but what could she do?

As Emily had feared, a scanner hung waist-high to the right of the emoto-vat door. Her badge most certainly was not programmed to provide access. In fact, it almost certainly would set off alarms. What had ever come over her, thinking she could come down here and get away with it? Now she'd almost certainly get fired, and then where would that leave her and Mark? Emily drew in a deep breath and tried to calm her nerves.

"Could you swipe me in?" Emily said, improvising as best as she could. She held up her badge, showing her head-shot and name. "I'm Emily Jones, and I'm supposed to check on one of the vats, but they messed up the reprogramming of my badge. You know. With the transfer and all."

Big Red stared at Emily and cocked her head to the side.

Emily waved the badge and pointed to the photo. "Emily Jones. See. I was working on the first floor."

"An Emotopath?" Big Red asked.

"One of the best," Emily said, finally telling the truth about something. "Senior Emotopath." Silence hung in the heavy air. Emily added, "They wanted me to see the entire operation. I think they have big plans for me." She grinned. "Although they probably won't give me a raise."

Big Red nodded thoughtfully, and after hesitating a few more seconds, she swiped her badge across the scanner. The heavy metal door opened, and Emily stepped inside the vast room. From left to right, it spanned the entire building's one hundred and fifty feet, and was about sixty feet deep. Floor-to-near-ceiling metal vats ran along each wall, side-by-side, with rubber tubing the size of fire hoses attached to the bottom and top of each. Electrical wiring entered the top of each vat. The smell of ozone filled the air.

Emily stood frozen. Like the proverbial dog who chases

a car with no idea of what to do once he catches it, Emily had no idea what to do next.

Although the hoses certainly looked inviting.

"You're not supposed to be here, are you?" Big Red said.

Emily opened her mouth, unsure of what to say, and then told the truth.

"My boyfriend and I," she began, "we need more of the good stuff than we can afford. He's my soulmate. I just know it. We get *so close* to each other, but then it wears off." Emily licked her dry lips. "But look at all of this! I don't know what's what, but this is enough for a lifetime. For both of us and both our lovers! Enough to keep an army of Emotopaths and you going for life. Without getting bled dry by the company."

But Big Red was backing away, eyes wide, shaking her head. And then she was gone out the door.

Alarm sirens shattered the silence.

———

FIGURING she had nothing more to lose, Emily sprinted to the nearest vat, leaped up and grabbed hold of the hose above her head. It pulled loose and Emily tumbled to the hard concrete floor. She looked up expectantly as red alarms strobed the air and sirens blared, but....

Nothing. Not a drop came from the exposed hose.

She ran to another vat, leaped up to grab another hose and...

A trickle of something moist dropped onto her face, but...

Emily felt nothing. For a few moments, at least.

Then, the floor began to shift beneath her feet. She didn't know what it represented, but it sure didn't equate to eternal soulmate status for her and Mark. Suddenly, it registered to her that the upper hoses had to be intake hoses filling the emoto-vat and the lower ones outtake, draining it.

Emily dropped to her knees and wrestled the nearest lower hose loose. A viscous dark fluid washed over her. Images of her and Mark flooded her mind. Walking along the beach, hand in hand. Kissing each other passionately. Her walking up the aisle of a church while an organ played "Here Comes the Bride," and Mark watched adoringly, clad in a black tuxedo.

The purest of the pure. This was it.

Emily laid down on the cold concrete and let it pour over her. She closed her eyes and wrapped her arms around her thoughts of Mark.

IT WAS SHEER BLISS. Emily didn't hear the sirens blare anymore or see the red alarm strobe lights. All she saw was her and Mark, together forever. The greatest of all soulmates.

Until the floor lifted her up. *You can't stay here.*

The viscous black fluid poured onto the floor, flooding it. Emily floated atop the fluid. Then atop a cushion of air atop the fluid.

Got to get you out.

Emily rolled over, splashing in the fluid, splashing it all

over her face, arms, and legs, but then felt herself lifted up above it again.

This place is killing you. You have to get out and never come back.

Emily screamed. Get out and never come back? Never! She smeared the fluid over her face, and over her breasts, and over her thighs. As she did, she felt Mark's loving hands doing the smearing, lingering lovingly on her breasts and thighs, then kissing her.

Taking you out of here.

"No!" Emily screamed.

She stumbled to her feet, fell, then crawled to the vat still spewing the fluid. Emily ducked her head in the flow and let it cascade over her until it ran dry. The fluid covered the floor, inches deep.

Get out! Get away from here!

But Emily wasn't going away. Not now. Not ever. She felt wonderful.

She stumbled to the next vat, and yanked loose the hose. And the next and the next. Let it all spill out.

Got to get you out!

Emily lay in the fluid, arms spread wide, beseeching Mark to join her. Come to me, my love. Come, my darling.

The fluid rose until it covered her chin, then her lips, and then almost her nose.

Got to save you. For your own good. Before it's too late.

The floor pulsed, lifting Emily up from the fluid, then dropping her back down again. And then it pulsed again.

As if finding its rhythm, the floor spasmed over and over, lifting Emily up and then down, slowly carrying her out the emoto-vat room's door.

"Let me go!" Emily cried. She got to her knees, but again the floor contracted and expanded, knocking her down, moving her down the corridor, toward the stairwell.

"No! You can't take this away from me!" she screamed, as Big Red and two other women raced passed her and disappeared into the stairwell.

The corridor walls joined the floor and ceiling, contracting and expanding, pulsing furiously. As Emily fought them, they blew the door off the stairwell.

Contracting and expanding, beating like a heart, they pushed Emily up the stairs with blasts of billowing air even as she fought to get back to the vats, the precious vats, and what they held for her and Mark.

"I've got to have it!"

Forget about Mark! Forget about soulmates!

The words—the blasphemy—turned Emily's blood cold. Shivers ran up and down her spine. Maybe, just maybe, Mark wasn't *the one.* If she couldn't get back and flood herself with more of that purest of pure Soulmate essence—and more importantly cover *him* with the essence —then perhaps he was a lost cause. Mark might not be her soulmate after all.

But she would never ever, ever, ever forget about finding her true soulmate. She would find him if it was the last thing she did. It was what gave her life meaning.

Forget about soulmates? Who would say such a horrible thing?

Somehow, Emily knew it was *the building* speaking such a blasphemy. It was *the factory*, perhaps a slaughter-house or a tannery in decades long past, and it held deep within itself the stains of blood and guts spilled long before she was even born.

It was this factory—*La fabrique d'amour*—that was trying to take away from her everything she cared about. She would never stop searching for her soulmate. Never!

You will or it will ruin you.

The pocket of air pulsed and pulsed, stronger and stronger, carrying her up to the first floor even as her arms flailed for purchase. It blew out the door and blew her out into the lobby.

Then it blew out all the doors. And blew her, tumbling, out the front door and onto the crumbling, weed-strewn sidewalk. The building contracted and expanded, ejecting one prisoner after another.

"I want it back!" Emily cried, thinking desperately of the black, viscous fluid that was the missing secret to her happiness.

You can't have it back. All of this was killing you.

Emily stared in disbelief as the building, its grimy, crumbling red brick exterior contracted and expanded like a beating heart.

Thump-thump, thump-thump.

Ejecting on a cushion of air one woman after another, and then an occasional man. Out the front doors. A crowd of them spilled onto the empty street and the side parking lot.

Thump-thump, thump-thump.

Emily ran crying for the front door, desperate to get back in and feel that viscous fluid pour over her again, make her feel *alive* and *in love* again. But the pulsating wind buffeted her, pushing her back, back, back. Giving her no more control of her body than if she were being carried by a tornado.

Thump-thump, thump-thump.

The crowd of employees stared in horror as the factory pulsed, spewing broken red bricks through the air.

It beat faster and faster, jackhammering with increasing force.

Thump-thump, thump-thump. Thump-thump, thump-thump.

Faster and faster still until finally, it ejected one last factory employee. One last prisoner.

You all are safe, now, the factory seemed to say to Emily. *You need be enslaved no longer.*

Emily knew she had been enslaved. A soulmate junkie. But she also knew that as soon as she could go back into that damned factory, she would run as fast as her legs could carry her, and she would immerse herself in whatever remained of that sweet black, viscous fluid that told her that she and Mark could be soulmates forevermore. Her life would have value, would have meaning. She would dive in the fluid and let it drown her, if need be.

Because it was all she had.

I will show you what true love really is. I will save you from yourself.

The heart of the building beat faster and faster, contracting more and more wildly. More crumpled bricks flew through the air as it spasmed and spasmed.

Faster and faster.

Until finally, the beating, brick heart collapsed in on

itself, imploding with an ear-splitting crash, sending plumes of crumbled bricks up into the sky, and filling the air with their dry smoke.

La fabrique d'amour—The Love Factory—beat no more.

THE BIRTH OF BOOGER NATION

INTRODUCTION TO THE BIRTH
OF BOOGER NATION

Blame this one on Dean Wesley Smith.

Dean edits and publishes *Pulphouse Fiction Magazine*, a legendary and unique publication I'm blessed to appear in regularly. It frequently includes imaginative yet edgy, bizarre stories that push genre expectations.

In a word, twisted.

I mean that in the best possible way. I often finish reading a *Pulphouse* story and say to myself, "Wow. That was amazing." You never read "same-old, same-old" in *Pulphouse*.

But then one day Dean decided to outdo himself and produce an anthology that pushed boundaries even further. Twisted wasn't enough. It would be called, *That's Really Messed Up: Whacked Out Stories from Pulphouse Fiction Magazine*. In other words, Dean wanted to take "twisted" to a whole new level.

Talk about waving a red flag in front of this bull.

"The Birth of Booger Nation" was the result of that challenge. Yeah, I out-twisted the great Dean Wesley Smith.

How exactly did this story emanate—or perhaps the more accurate verb would be *ooze*—from my creative subconscious? I'll be damned if I know. Sometimes (often!) I'm convinced that I'm better off not knowing.

Another editor who read the story shook his head and responded, "Hendrickson, what the hell is wrong with you?"

A damned fine question. And totally unanswerable.

But I'll also note that the very same editor said he'd buy the story in a heartbeat. Sometimes, being just a little bit nuts—or a whole lotta nuts—can be a good thing.

Or as Dean wrote in his *That's Really Messed Up* introduction to the story, "I am fairly certain this story is science fiction unless there is a genre called 'head-shaking.' This story has to be both."

THE BIRTH OF BOOGER NATION

For millions and millions of years, boogers were just boogers. They were a fragment of dirt, or some other impurity, caught by human nose hairs and enveloped in mucus to prevent the dirt from reaching human lungs.

Nothing more, nothing less.

Dirt or other inorganic particles combined with organic mucus. With no more ability to think than the lifeless dirt at their center.

It took what humans consider a truly gross act—you thought you were getting Fyodor Dostoyevsky here, or a Pulitzer Prize nominee?—to breathe sentience into the first booger.

Into us.

On our first day of creation decades ago, Tommy McLeod, a thin, eleven-year-old human with wavy black hair and the beginnings of teenage acne, sat at the desk in his bedroom playing a video game. His nose twitched. And then it twitched some more. No matter how much he tried to concentrate on the game, his nose kept distracting him.

Twitch. Twitch. Twitch.

Finally, he put the game on pause and went on a mining expedition. He plunged his index finger up his nose, wriggled it around, and came out with the culprit, a big, juicy one. Then quite without thinking, he ate it.

Eeew, gross! you say?

Humans may be disgusted by the act, but for boogers everywhere Tommy McLeod became Father Booger and his act became a sacrament. The more creative among us have speculated that this first seed for all sentient boogers to follow might well have offered a delicate bouquet and a taste with a hint of cedar and citrus. Their critics, of course, note that there is no way to know, and in any case, such a sacrament should not be reduced to a matter of cuisine.

Whatever the case, Booger Adam had been created.

At about the same time and in the same city in Northern Florida, and in much the same fashion, Carla Thompson, fifteen years old with long, brown hair and an often sad smile, created Booger Eve. Is it fair that we'll respect Carla's privacy and offer fewer details of her own mining expedition and subsequent consumption of her own juicy morsel, save to say that she was reading a book at the time? Well, even the least advanced of boogers can tell that teenage human girls have a tougher time of it than boys, so we'll simply acknowledge Carla's role as Mother Booger, praise and honor her, and leave it at that.

Booger scientists laboring in laboratories in moist, hair-filled nasal passages across the world don't know for sure what happened next. They can only theorize that two events combined to form the Booger Big Bang.

First, unknown actions involving the unique enzymes in the stomachs of Mother and Father Booger produced important mutations in the resulting kernels of the boogers. And then, somehow, those mutated kernels met in the hundred million, billion-to-one longshot that created Booger Nation.

Clearly, the booger kernels had to be excreted to somehow meet and produce their progeny. Much speculation has occurred since there is no known record of Tommy and Carla ever having actually met or even known of each other's existence. Unfortunately, the likeliest explanation is also the most disgusting, at least to human sensibilities. That said, there are no known delicate forms of excretion.

As a result, the more timid among you should happily skip to the next paragraph and move on with this accounting of our birth. Those who remain—most of you possessing the same motivation as those who gawk at highway accidents—will be spared the worst of the descriptive details and will have to suffice with the explanation that both were known to frequent a small lake near their city, and at that lake there were—it isn't too late to skip ahead to the next paragraph—Port-a-Potties.

You can't say you weren't warned.

However the two magical kernels may have met, the resulting explosion is what we have since called the Booger Big Bang. Billions and billions of tiny particles that looked like dirt but were far, far more than dirt—they were *aware*—blew in the wind and became lodged amidst the hairs in moist human nasal passages.

Whenever two such particles met and merged, the level of sentience exploded orders and orders of magnitude. Such coupling is a wonderful thing for our collective consciousness to experience. The probing. The acceptance. The two becoming one. But a one almost infinitely greater than the sum of its parts.

To humans, it may appear as nothing more than two boogers humping each other. But for us it is a sacred act.

And because we multiply so rapidly, we have grown almost overnight from a consciousness barely above that of an amoeba to one that far surpasses you humans. Frankly, it amazes us that some of you can even manage to get out of bed in the morning and land on your feet. But you are useful hosts, and so we tolerate you.

(The less discreet citizens of Booger Nation, however, cannot help but make fun of you. And if you think *we* look funny humping each other, you should take a cold, hard look at yourselves someday.)

Boogers everywhere cherish the hope that one day, the Carl Sagan of our kind will narrate a documentary called *Booger Cosmos* and in it explain to humans the profound event of the Booger Big Bang and how it led to billions and billions of sentient boogers. Those of us with connections in the entertainment industry—do you doubt they exist?— are convinced that while the show might not generate great ratings, it will at least make it to Netflix.

Your doubt is palpable.

How do we know all this? How could we *ever* have discovered everything from the events involving our mother, Carla Thompson, and our father, Tommy McLeod, to their excreted kernels meeting in our big bang?

Our devout say this is part of our collective unconscious and we just *know*. Our skeptics say that like human creation stories, it's all made up, it makes no sense, and only a fool would believe it. But it's still the best we have.

Either way, we're here to stay.

We will no longer be mere unthinking, annoying blobs in your nasal passages. There is no putting this, as you would say, "genie back in the bottle." In an unimaginably short time, we have not only become aware, we have surpassed you.

If we really cared what you thought of us, we would ask —no, demand—that you call us *nasal crusts* instead of boogers.

But Booger Nation is proud of what it is. We are proud of what we are, and even more importantly, we can only imagine what we will someday become. We are proud to be boogers and want no other name.

With or without you, we will expand into space.

We will travel to the stars.

We are sure that we are not alone.

STEPPING INTO THE LIGHT

INTRODUCTION TO STEPPING INTO THE LIGHT

Welcome to Cave Creek, a mythical old mining town north of Las Vegas where impossible things happen. Dean Wesley Smith created this fictional town and has to date released four books in the series: his novel *Card Sharp Silver*, and three related anthologies, *Bitter Mountain Moonlight* (Past), *Open Ended Threat* (Present), and *Promise in the Gold* (Future).

My story "The Run of Her Life" concluded *Open Ended Threat* (and is available in my recently released collection *Cape Cod Chips, Wiener Dogs, and Swiping Left: Stories of Sweet Romance*). The story you're about to read appeared in *Bitter Mountain Moonlight*.

"Stepping Into the Light" was a wonderful learning experience. For starters, I'd never before written a Western. Well, if you're going to write a story set over a hundred years ago in an old Nevada mining town ... that story is going to be, pretty much by definition, a Western, albeit one with a strong element of the fantastic.

I wasn't about to let that stop me. I can be stubborn to

the point of absurdity in many negative ways, but when it involves pursuing an important goal, that stubbornness transforms itself into tenacious determination.

And I desperately wanted to write this story. So that whole "I've never before written a Western" thing wasn't an insurmountable obstacle. It was an opportunity. A challenge I embraced.

I began by watching the forty-one videos in WMG Publishing's online course in writing Westerns. Not just watching. Studying. Taking copious notes. Then I continued the research I'd already begun while writing "The Run of Her Life" into the Cave Creek mythos and details concerning that area of Nevada in the early 1900s. All the while, I tossed ideas around in my head.

Does that seem like a whole lot of work for one little old story? Hey, it ain't work if you're having fun. And the thing about learning is that it's never wasted. It always goes into the cauldron for heating up the next tasty stew.

For whatever reason, I haven't yet written another Western, but it feels inevitable that I will someday. Especially when I recall what a great time I had writing this story.

STEPPING INTO THE LIGHT

October 8, 1915
Cave Creek, Nevada

Mabel Hardman guided the staggering, drunken miner named Henry as best she could down the dusty Main Street, trying her best to avoid the clumps of fresh horse manure. It was a challenge. The wide dirt road was dimly lit by moonlight, irregularly placed lanterns casting off their gloomy glow, and light spilling out of the raucous saloons and gambling houses where pianos played and men hooted and hollered.

Mabel looped Henry's left arm over her shoulder and wrapped her right arm around his back, pinning their sides together. At five-feet tall and a hundred and thirty pounds, she was no match for his size. He towered eight or nine inches over her and outweighed her by fifty or sixty pounds with thick, meaty forearms. Each time he stumbled, he threatened to take the two of them down together, potentially face first into a steaming pile of manure.

But this wasn't Mabel Hardman's first rodeo. She was no child. She was twenty-one years old and strong for her size. She kept him moving. He reeked of sweat and whiskey with a hint of vomit, but she expected that. The men always did. She hardly smelled sweet herself. Cave Creek was a long way from any natural springs to bathe in. As long as she and Henry didn't add any horse manure to their boots—and Henry didn't vomit—Mabel would be happy.

Or as happy as a working girl in a mining town like Cave Creek ever got.

She'd gotten payment as soon as the two of them stepped outside of the Wild Stallion saloon and tucked it into the hidden side pocket sewn into her best working dress, the one that puffed up her unimpressive breasts as best as possible and was cut low enough to show most of what she had. Most men hardly considered her the pick of the litter, not with her homely face and tiny bosom, but some did like her fire-red hair.

"That head of yours gets me to burning!" Henry had said back at the saloon, then burst into uproarious laughter at his clever wit. Soon he was taking two last belts of whiskey and they were walking out the door.

No one had bothered them as they'd walked along Main Street, as wide as about four or five stagecoaches front to back, lined with wooden buildings housing the general store, an apothecary, the countless saloons and gambling houses, and the Golden Dream Hotel. There'd been no need to reach for the sharp, long knife in a leather sheath strapped to her left calf. In fact, there had been other working girls walking with their own customers ahead of and behind them on the way to their cribs.

Just another night in Cave Creek.

Even so, Mabel shivered. Not because of any chill in the air for there was none. In fact, the air this time of night felt quite pleasant after the oppressive heat during the day when women of her kind slept. Her shiver also had nothing to do with her task at hand. She'd done it so many times by now, she'd learned to retreat into the darkness of her mind even as the man with her performed his actions in the darkness of her bed.

Her shiver came not from fear or chill or shame. It was merely a foreboding that something bad was about to happen. This wasn't the first time, and more often than not, she shook her head the next day at her silliness, seeing ghosts and apparitions where there were none.

But strange things did happen in Cave Creek. Sometimes, Mabel's ghostly shivers proved to be well founded. It was a strange place to live. And a quite horrible place for a working girl like her, although she supposed any place would be quite horrible to live this life.

Her best friend, Daisy O'Shea, whose crib was right next to Mabel's—Daisy was really Mabel's *only* friend—had talked in recent days and weeks of fleeing Cave Creek and this life, sinking deeper and deeper into despondency and such melancholia that the men couldn't bear to be around her unless they were falling down drunk or pumping their seed into her and couldn't have cared if she had fainted dead away.

But where could women like them go?

Nowhere.

They both knew that answer. The difference was that Mabel accepted her fate; Daisy couldn't. Or wouldn't. She might even be going mad. She hadn't been among the other working girls walking with customers on the street, and she hadn't been back at the Wild Stallion, so Mabel made a mental note to check on her when Henry finished what he'd paid to do.

They turned off Main Street and stumbled through the sudden darkness toward her two-room crib, a rickety, wooden shack in a row of ten such cribs, each with a bedroom barely large enough for a bed in front and an even smaller kitchen in back.

"You're *shoooo bootiful*," Henry said, slurring almost all his words now that his final belts of whiskey had hit home. Then he bent over and vomited, splattering both of their boots.

Mabel clenched her eyes shut and grimaced as Henry spewed a fountain of noxious liquids for what felt like a very long time.

That was her life, she thought. Clenching her eyes and grimacing as unpleasant acts went on for a very long time—for what often felt like forever—was exactly what she did.

She certainly hadn't planned to be a working girl. Who did? But she'd been poor and naïve—*a fool!*—and a devil named Eli Crawford had taken advantage of her and ruined her forever. When her father found out, he'd blamed her and disowned her. Sent her packing, penniless, on a stagecoach to Las Vegas from where, in dazed bewilderment, she continued on to Cave Creek.

Where money was flowing.

With the Great War going on in Europe, albeit without hardly any American boys, "the war to end all wars" had turned Cave Creek into a boomtown. Wartime demand for minerals was great for business, especially copper production.

Opportunities galore. For men with money. For men without money. Even opportunities for women of stature who had not been ruined.

But no opportunities for ruined women. No opportunities except one.

So now, this was the life that Mabel led.

In so many ways, it was a life that couldn't get over soon enough.

"*Shorry*," Henry said when his stomach finally stopped erupting.

He spat, wiped his mouth off with his shirt sleeve, then spat again. The air smelled even more unspeakably foul than usual.

They went inside her crib. Henry complained about using a cap as did so many others, but he complied and mercifully completed the act without further stomach eruption.

Mabel stood before Daisy's crib, her sense of foreboding mounting. The pitch black darkness was broken only by the moonlight; the lanterns on Main Street and the escaping light from its raucous establishments did not reach the cribs. No sound escaped through the shack's thin walls. No rustling of clothing, grunts or murmurs, words, or even the weeping Mabel had heard all too often from within.

The simple explanation for the silence was that Daisy was at one of the saloons working, and she'd be back soon with a customer. But she always worked at the Wild Stallion, nowhere else, and she hadn't been there all night.

Something also smelled faintly wrong. Faint, but foul.

Mabel knocked on the door. "Daisy?" she called softly.

No answer.

Mabel waited. If Daisy were in there with a customer, albeit an unbelievably quiet one, it would be a terrible offense to interrupt.

But could any man be that quiet? The bed was just on the other side of the thin walls.

Mabel knocked again. Called out Daisy's name again.

A horse tied up at the far left end of the row of cribs whinnied. A man inside another crib halfway down grunted and roared his pleasure as he completed the act he'd paid for.

But still no answer from inside Daisy's crib.

Mabel opened the door a crack. The foul stench of urine and feces hit her. She staggered back as a cloud of flies swarmed out.

Something was wrong. Very wrong.

Mabel dashed back inside her own crib, lighted the wick on her lantern and carried it back to Daisy's door. Bracing herself against the horrible stench, she opened the door and as the lantern's flickering candle cast its meager light, she peered inside.

And saw the deathly sight on the bed.

Mabel cried out. Almost dropping the lantern, she staggered back.

Daisy lay on her back in a white nightdress, mouth open in death, her frail, thin arms flung out as if in despair.

Flies buzzed all about her pallid form. In death, she had soiled herself.

Mabel stepped cautiously inside. Touched Daisy's cold neck to be sure of her death, and choked back a sob.

Only then did she see the empty container of arsenic lying beside Daisy's lifeless form.

MABEL WAITED outside the crib at the far end of the row where the horse was tied to a wooden post. She stared at her shaking hands, clasping and unclasping them.

Daisy was gone.

What could have been done to stop her? Mabel didn't know. She knew only that she had failed her one and only friend. Failed to stop her from taking her own life.

Not that the very same thought hadn't occurred to Mabel herself. She supposed it was yet another part of a working girl's life.

The life of a whore.

There it was. She'd said it, at least in her mind. *She was a whore. Daisy was a whore. Or at least* had been *a whore.* To hell with the "working girl" euphemism.

Not a part of polite society. Or even truly a part of the crude miner's society.

Mabel had no idea if the powers that be in Cave Creek would allow Daisy to be buried in their cemetery, but Mabel doubted it. Even then, "decent" townspeople would just spit on that desecrated ground. Almost certainly, the best Daisy would get would be an unmarked grave out in the desert. She'd possibly just be left out there to rot and be torn apart by wild animals.

Well, dammit, Daisy deserved better.

All the "good" townspeople would have had no better luck finding a means of survival had they been thrust into the lives of Daisy, Mabel, or the other working girls. Mabel would not allow Daisy's memory to be spat upon. She would find a place out in the desert, a nice place that Daisy would have liked, that would become her final resting place. Mabel would give her a proper burial and visit her often.

It would be their secret. No one else's to tarnish or sully with even a hint of a bad thing to say about the poor girl.

The crib door opened, startling Mabel into a yelp.

"What the hell are you doing here?" demanded the man, scowling.

Mabel recognized him, though she wasn't sure of his name. Johnson? Randall Johnson? Yes, that was it. Thin and wiry, about forty years old with thinning gray hair. One of the town's barbers. Married, she thought.

Behind him appeared the girl he'd visited. Edith Langston. Frowning, with the same question as her customer written all over her face.

"Sir, I'd like to borrow your horse," Mabel said, staring at the ground. "It's an emergency."

"Absolutely not!" he thundered. "Now get out of my way!"

"I'll pay you, sir."

His scowl lightened. "How much?"

Mabel quoted the usual price of her services. It would wipe out what she'd made from Henry, and she'd be making no more money tonight, but it would be worth it. "And I'll have it back before sunrise."

"And if you don't?"

Mabel blinked. She hadn't thought that far ahead. "Why, you can have me hung as a horse thief."

"Double your price and show me some gratitude in the future," Randall Johnson said, "and you've got a deal."

MABEL LED THE HORSE, a sturdy chestnut, west from the cribs over a series of rises until she found what she considered the perfect spot. It was up against a rock outcropping that towered thirty feet high and curved in a semicircle that Mabel, knowing she was overcome with emotion, took to be embracing arms.

She had cleaned Daisy up as much as possible, dressed her in her favorite dress and a white bonnet, then gently slung her over the saddle and strapped her in along with a scavenged shovel. The shovel, like the horse, would need to be back before sunrise.

As Mabel had walked alongside the horse, reins in hand, their steps illuminated by nothing other than moonlight, her heart had skipped a beat every time a wild animal howled or something rustled in the scrub. She'd stopped fearing death a long time ago. She just didn't want it to come by way of a wild pack of wolves tearing her apart, chomping noisily on whatever they considered her most succulent parts. The horse hadn't exactly been crazy about being out here either. Mabel had had to hold tight to the reins a couple times to make sure it didn't bolt.

But they'd made it to this most perfect spot with the stars twinkling brightly in the clear sky. Mabel knew she was sentimentalizing the embracing arms of the rock outcropping. She more than anyone should have not a single ounce of sentiment left in her body. Not a speck.

And she didn't. Not for herself. But she did for Daisy. Who'd just been too damned sweet for her own good.

Mabel tied the horse to a clump of rocks in the shape of a jagged post on the left edge of the embracing arms, then unstrapped Daisy and the shovel.

Mabel figured she'd speak her words about Daisy first, then dig. She'd been thinking of her words all the way out here, and figured they were best spoken while she was as fresh as possible and not worn out from digging Daisy's grave.

Carrying Daisy and staggering beneath the dead weight, Mabel moved to the middle of the embracing arms, twenty feet back from the rock face. She dropped to one knee, and was about to set Daisy down onto her final resting place and begin the eulogy when the air began to hum all about them.

Mabel felt her arms, a split second before so weary she had feared dropping Daisy, lighten as if she carried the burden no longer. Sparks of light flickered inches from her face. And then bright, white midday light burst through an oval shape barely more than her height and width and just a step away.

As if in a trance, Mabel stepped forward with Daisy and into the light.

MABEL'S JAW DROPPED. She couldn't believe her eyes.

What had happened?

The late afternoon sun beamed brightly overhead while just a moment before she'd stood in pitch black darkness. Oppressive heat blasted like a furnace sending salty sweat into her eyes while just a moment before she'd stood in the midnight coolness.

And that was the least of it.

She stood, holding Daisy in her arms, on a grassy, rock-strewn hillside overlooking a wide paved roadway where sleek automobiles that looked nothing like the Model T flew by in both directions at horrifying speeds. More of the automobiles parked around bright-colored buildings of sorts with names like McDonalds, Wendy's, and Pizza Hut.

What was a McDonald's? And what were those golden arches for? Who was Wendy? A working girl? No, that couldn't be. There were women and children going in and out of the place. And what was pizza?

High overhead was a huge, silver metal thing—an airplane!—flying through the air. But it was nothing like what Mabel had seen in the newspapers. This was sleek, silver, and solid. And with no propellers! How could it move? More importantly, weren't almost all the airplanes reserved for fighting in the war? This wasn't Germany or France or Austria or wherever it was in Europe that the world was fighting the war to end all wars. This was Cave Creek, Nevada.

Or was it?

This was most definitely *not* Cave Creek. The familiar mountains still rose in the West, and Cave Creek's sweltering midday heat still sucked the air out of her lungs.

But this was not Cave Creek.

Was the silver airplane above a German airplane that had somehow flown all the way across the ocean and was about to bomb this not-Cave-Creek place? It was a crazy thought, but Mabel ducked down and moved a few steps to her right to the cover of a green shrub brush. She laid the suddenly heavy body of Daisy on the coarse grass beneath the overhanding branches of the shrubs.

Where was this? What *was this?*

She glanced back up at the airplane.

No bombs.

Her eyes returned to the paved roadway and the astonishing speeds of the automobiles. Were these automobiles racing back and forth as part of the war effort?

And what of the people going in and out of the places like McDonald's? The women were barely clothed! Mabel felt embarrassed for them. Not even a working girl like her showed that much bare skin. They were walking around half naked! And some of their trousers were torn to shreds yet they wore them anyway.

What a strange, strange place!

And certainly not Cave Creek.

A rustling noise sounded from the thick brush off to the right.

Mabel tensed. She had to hide. *They* had to hide. She wasn't leaving Daisy behind for whomever it was that was approaching.

Mabel looked back to her left, just a few steps away, where she had stood when she first stepped into the light. A black oval remained of the same shape and size of the one filled with light that she'd entered. She'd been so astonished at these amazing sights, she'd never looked behind her at the dark.

Mabel scooped up Daisy, grunted at the dead weight, stepped toward the dark, and—

--tripped on a loose, foot-sized rock, stumbled, and—

--dropped Daisy, and—

--toppled into the dark.

Alone.

Mabel whirled back around.

She lunged for the light.

Too late.

It had winked out.

On her knees, Mabel pawed about for the light. She had to find it! She had to get Daisy!

But the light was gone.

MABEL SEARCHED for hours on her knees, bewildered and crying salty tears for the first time since her first few months as a working girl. But there was no light. And no Daisy.

Finally, fearing the wrath of the horse- and shovel-owners, Mabel mounted the chestnut and raced back, beating sunrise by scant minutes. She had hated herself ever since she allowed that devil Eli Crawford destroy her world, but Mabel now found new depths for that hatred.

She despised herself. She had failed Daisy in her final hour. What kind of friend did that?

Perhaps, Mabel thought, she should empty a container of arsenic herself.

THE NEXT NIGHT, Mabel returned to the embracing arms, finding it without difficulty. She needed no horse or shovel. No Daisy this time to transport. No need to dig a grave.

Mabel came to think of Daisy. And the darkness that had overcame her and had eventually consumed her.

Mabel also came to wait for the light. Just in case.

That oval shape had appeared once and taken her in. Perhaps at the same time this evening, it would take her in again. And she could retrieve Daisy. If there was a Daisy to retrieve.

If there was, Mabel would dig a grave with her own hands. Perhaps one for both of them.

Perhaps here in the dark. Perhaps in the light.

And if instead, a wild pack of wolves tore her to pieces, Mabel doubted she'd even scream.

THE LIGHT DID INDEED APPEAR. At the same time and place as the night before, as best Mabel could tell, and scant moments after she'd completed speaking Daisy's overdue eulogy.

In the pitch black darkness, the air began to hum. Sparks of light flickered. And then the brightest of white light burst through the hoped-for oval shape.

Mabel dove through it.

She landed on all fours in the same grassy, rock-strewn hillside as before, baking almost instantly in the furnace-like heat, and looking down on the terrifying roadway.

But there was no Daisy.

Mabel cried out. She tried to hold back her sorrow and anger, but could not. She burst into uncontrollable, wracking sobs. Grief for betraying her friend.

Her one and only friend. Now gone.

"We're sorry about your friend," a voice behind her said somberly.

Mabel whirled and leapt to her feet. "Who are you? What have you done with Daisy?"

Two women, both clean-looking with long, untangled hair and smelling peculiarly like flowers, stood before her. Instead of dresses, they wore the same strange clothing Mabel had seen on those who walked in and out of those strange places near the roadway. McDonald's. Wendy's. Pizza Hut. Although these women had no shredded trousers on their legs. Theirs looked practically new. And they showed less skin, for whatever reason.

"I'm Jeanne," said the short one with black hair. About Mabel's own height, five foot even. Skinny as a rail. Looked like she'd missed a lot of meals, but she smiled pleasantly.

"I'm Linda," said the other, a good six inches taller and not quite as starved-looking, but still hardly of sturdy stock. They both looked like they could get blown over by a good gust of wind.

"What have you done with Daisy?" Mabel demanded.

"She was dead," the one named Jeanne said gently. "You do know that, right?"

"Of course! But that still gives you no right to steal her body. I want it back so I can give her a proper burial"—

Mabel point at the dark oval—"back there. Back in the dark where we belong."

"It isn't that easy," said the taller one, Linda. "You see, while only a single day went by in your time, on the other side of that portal"—she pointed to the dark oval—"a week passed here. You would not have wanted us to leave her body here for you. Not for that long. We had to take it away."

Mabel couldn't speak. Her mind suddenly would not work, spinning wildly out of control. She felt herself growing dizzy.

The two women moved to her side. Each took an elbow and steadied her.

"It's okay," the one called Jeanne said. "We know this is difficult."

Somewhere, in the foggy recesses of her mind, Mabel heard herself ask, "What did you do with Daisy?"

WHEN MABEL REFUSED to talk of anything else, they brought her to see Daisy's body. The two women led her down a winding secluded path that seemed to take far longer than necessary, looked all around to make sure no one could see them—reminding Mabel of a cheating husband trying to hide his dirty secret—then loaded her into the back seat of a huge, black automobile with dark windows so no one could look inside.

The automobile was very comfortable, even with the strap pulled around her and clicked at her hip. Mabel sat directly behind Linda, who drove, while Jeanne sat in the back with her and tried to explain the situation.

But it made no sense at all.

This was 2021? And this was still Cave Creek, but more than a century had passed? Just by her stepping into the light, what Jeanne called a portal? And when Mabel stepped back into the dark, the portal took her back into 1915? And now she'd have to wait a week, as they measured time here, before she could go back? But she'd only have missed a day back in her old time?

Who could believe such nonsense?

"Are you making fun of me?" Mabel finally asked.

Jeanne smiled weakly. "Not at all. It's the truth, even though it is hard to believe. Linda and I are part of a council here that helps people like you. Explains things and makes sure everything works out for the best."

Mabel wasn't sure what it meant for things to work out for the best. Usually when townspeople said things like that, things didn't work out very well for girls like her.

"You're taking me to Daisy?"

"Yes, we promised," Jeanne said.

"You better not be lying."

"We aren't," Jeanne said softly and patted Mabel's hand.

Suddenly, Mabel sat bolt upright. "Why are you taking me here?" The sign read the Golden Dream Hotel. Mabel knew full well this was a place where she was not welcome. No working girls were allowed on the premises. It was unthinkable.

"It's okay," Jeanne said soothingly.

"No it isn't! I'll be arrested. Is that what all this about?

You've tricked me into getting arrested?" Mabel's heart pounded. And to think she had actually begun to trust these two women. She could only imagine what they had planned for her.

Not that her life could get any worse.

"You aren't going to be arrested or anything of the sort," Jeanne explained in that soothing tone that Mabel had begun to believe in. "But we do need to keep you a secret for a while."

"Why?" Mabel asked. "I mean, I understand you being ashamed of me. I've dealt with that since... well, for a very long time."

"We're not ashamed of you at all. Personally, I'm proud of you and Linda is too."

"I'm a *whore*," Mabel said. "I know what I am. I don't need to be lied to. You don't need to tell me you love me. Just give me your damned money!" She swallowed a bitter taste from her mouth.

"It isn't that at all," Jeanne said. "We really are proud of you. But we need to keep the portals a secret. Only a small number of us—the council—know about it. We need to keep it that way. That's why we were waiting for you when you arrived this time. Not because we're ashamed of you. But for right now, we need to keep you a secret."

Mabel let all of that sink in.

Linda pulled the automobile into what felt like a dark tunnel. She turned on bright lights that guided her way, around curves that led them down deeper into what was apparently an underground garage.

Not as far underground as the miners, of course. But further than Mabel had ever gone.

Linda pulled up to a door, and dropped the two of them off.

"I'll see you inside," she said.

***

AFTER TAKING A RIGHT JUST inside the garage door, and then a left, they came to an unmarked locked room. Jeanne fished a key out of her pocket, opened the door, turned on the lights, led Mabel inside, and locked the door behind them.

A large dark wood table with twelve matching chairs filled most of the room. Dark wood paneling covered the walls. At the far end stood a closed casket.

"We had to guess what you wanted," Jeanne said. "We did our best."

A lump formed in Mabel's throat.

"Based on customs in 1915, we had Daisy embalmed," Jeanne said. "You'll be able to see her close to the way she was before her death. These days, however, many choose cremation."

"You will not burn Daisy!" Mabel said, panic rising in her voice. "Everyone knows girls like us are going to Hell where we're going to burn, but you are *not* going to burn Daisy!"

"That's what we figured you would say," Jeanne said. "That's why we had her embalmed. But we can review all your options later. For now, you may view the body."

MABEL, Jeanne, and Linda sat at a round, dark wood table in a small nearby office, once again with matching dark wood paneling.

"You can have Daisy buried here," Linda said, "but if you want her remains to go back to 1915, it will be very difficult to get a casket back up that hill and in through the portal without being detected. And we can't allow that to happen."

Jeanne put a warm hand over Mabel's. "But if you change your mind about cremation—"

"I won't!" Mabel insisted.

"If you do," Jeanne said. "you can bring an urn with her ashes through the portal. Perhaps sprinkle those ashes in that special place for her."

"You have a week to think about it," Linda said. "It's either burial here in 2021—and we would require some secrecy—or take her ashes back to 1915."

"No ashes," Mabel said, shaking her head. "No ashes."

"Okay, then there's the matter of you," Jeanne said.

"What about me?" Mabel said, her sadness turning to alarm. "I don't want to burn either."

"No, no, nothing like that," Jeanne said, and patted her hand again. "We aren't equipped to have everyone leave their original time and stay here permanently. It would be impossible to maintain secrecy.

"But in some cases, we are able to build a cover story for someone, establish an official identity, and set them up with a new life here in 2021. We could do that for you."

Mabel stared at them, unable to speak.

"It would be entirely your choice," Jeanne said. "You would be able to live in my guest bedroom."

"What would I do?" Mabel asked, totally bewildered.

"Whatever you choose," Jeanne said.

"As long as it's different from what you've been doing," Linda said. "You have a sponsor to cover the expenses, but she's motivated to get you out of the life you're living now and into a better one here in 2021."

"You have a week before the portal opens again," Jeannie said. "Think about it. You'll be staying with me. My house is secluded so it's ideal. We can talk about any questions you have."

THE NEXT DAY OVER LUNCH, after taking the most amazing hot shower she ever could have imagined, Mabel asked two questions. She tried not to be totally distracted by eating the mouth-watering slices of the thing they called pizza, presumably from that Hut place out on the roadway. But it was so delicious—by far the most wonderful thing she'd ever tasted—that Mabel had to set it aside so she could concentrate. Even then, the smell was impossible to ignore.

"What if I wanted to go back just a little bit earlier than my time?" she asked as Jeanne smiled warmly from the other side of the plain kitchen table. A window looked out on a thick wooded area, buttressing her claim of a secluded area. "What I mean is," Mabel said frowning, "could I go back to August or September of 1915 instead of October. Could I do that?"

Jeanne nodded. "There are many portals to many times. There certainly aren't so many that you can pick a specific date and time to go back to, but yes, you could step into a portal that would take you back to an earlier time." She cocked her head. "Why?"

"I want to save Daisy," Mabel said, her hope rising. "I want to go back early enough so I can help her and keep her from wanting to kill herself. There's got to be something I could do for her."

A sad look came over Jeanne's pleasant face. She shook her head.

"That isn't how it works," she said. "In your timeline, she's dead and you can't change that. There are many timelines, and with each decision a new timeline branches off. So there are timelines where Daisy doesn't kill herself, but you can't change what has already happened in yours. I'm sorry."

Mabel's heart sank. She'd thought for a moment there that she could somehow bring Daisy back from the dead.

But there was no bringing her back.

Mabel reached for another slice of pizza. There was no need to worry anymore about being distracted. She needed some distraction after that answer.

"What was your other question?" Jeanne asked.

Mabel took a bite, chewed, then set the pizza down.

"I guess it was pretty much the same question," she said. "A man named Eli Crawford did a very bad thing to me. A wicked thing. He ruined me. So I guess I was wondering if I could go back in time and stop him somehow." The thought had flashed through Mabel's mind that she'd even consider killing him. He *deserved* to be killed for what he'd done. But she wasn't about to admit that to this kind woman who'd welcomed her into her home. "Maybe then I'd live the life I was meant to live. And not end up in Cave Creek. *As a whore.*"

She spat the last words out bitterly, but she hadn't been able to stop herself. The words had needed to be said.

Jeanne held Mabel's hand.

"No, you can't go back and stop him. But what you can do, here in 2021, is try again to live that life you were meant to live."

———

MABEL STOOD ON THE GRASSY, rock-strewn hillside, and stepped through the portal. Into the dark. She carried the silver-colored urn that held Daisy's ashes. Daisy would never live in this strange world of 2021, so she deserved to go home where she belonged.

To those embracing arms Mabel had found for her.

Mabel swung the urn from side to side. The ashes flew through the air, barely visible in the meager moonlight. High above, the stars twinkled in the clear sky.

Mabel hoped Daisy found a peace in this special resting place, a peace she had not found in life.

When the ashes were gone and the urn emptied, Mabel stepped back into the light where she would stay. This world was terrifying and intoxicating at the same time.

But she had nothing to lose. And everything to gain.

Perhaps, after all, she could still live the life she'd been meant to live.

LOST BALLS

INTRODUCTION TO LOST BALLS

I take workshops all the time. Writing is one endeavor where there's always something to learn. Much like great white sharks, writers have to keep moving forward or they creatively die. (Admittedly, it has been suggested that the better shark analogy for me would be a hammerhead.)

A Cross Genre workshop prompted me to write this story. Some genres might be impossible to combine, but I'll argue that humor and fantasy are a match made in heaven. That combination is very much in my wheelhouse. Small wonder that it was my cross-genre choice for that workshop's assigned story.

How did this particular idea pop into my head? In retrospect, it feels like an intuitively obvious one. But in truth, I must once again shrug my shoulders, shake my befuddled head, and say, "Not a clue."

LOST BALLS

Jimmy O'Malley knew he deserved it, but it didn't make the reality any easier to take. His wife, Helen, had taken away his balls and put them in her purse.

Not figuratively. Literally.

Not a mere comedian's punchline. For real.

Not his golf balls or his baseballs or his basketballs.

His balls balls. His *my-ding-a-ling* balls.

The balls *formerly* belonging to him. That used to be tucked inside tighty-whities that were now sadly and quite shockingly spacious.

Balls that now belonged to Helen, secured safely away in her beige, knock-off Louis Vuitton purse.

And it was all his fault.

Jimmy pushed the old, beat-up lawnmower through the jungle of the backyard lawn, a raging hangover grasping his skull and crushing it into crumbling eggshells, his poor head tortured by the roaring lawnmower, the sickening smell of gasoline, and the Saturday morning sun still low enough on the horizon to drive slivers of bright light into his eyeballs every time he turned and faced the right side of the lot.

What the hell had happened to his life?

The lawnmower coughed, sputtered, and died—for what was now a fifth time—as it hit a too-thick clump of grass mixed with weeds and fallen dead leaves left over from the fall. Jimmy silently cursed. Sweat drenched his mop of thick brown hair. It slid down his forehead and face, stinging his eyes and tasting salty on his lips. His sopping-wet, faded Red Sox World Series T-shirt clung to his sagging gut. Wincing, he grasped the black plastic handle to the pull cord, tilted the lawnmower up to free it from the grass, and yanked to bring the engine roaring back to painful life even as he dreamed of the bliss of a quick death.

He couldn't exactly blame Helen, his wife of three years. A software whiz for a Fortune 500 company and made more money than he did down at the plant. A lot more. Good looking though not exactly a bombshell. Long auburn hair. Glasses. A clear complexion, pretty green eyes, and a nice smile. Permanently ten pounds overweight, according to her, an assessment he'd one time had the misfortune to verbally agree with.

Nope, this was not her fault. The blame was all his. His poker night with the boys had turned into a trip to a local strip joint and after several rounds of shots, things had gotten a little crazy and then things had gotten a lot crazy, ending in a fight with a bouncer twice his size and then his arrest.

Not that he could remember any of it. It might help him get through this nightmare if he could at least recall the good parts—there had surely been good parts, hadn't there? —but all pleasures were denied him now.

Helen had bailed him out at the police station with a look that even in his obliterated state Jimmy knew meant big-time trouble if not outright war. He might be sleeping on the couch for the next year. He might have to wait till the next century for sex.

But it was worse than that. At some point during the night, Helen had confiscated his balls.

He'd awoken to his jackhammer of a hangover, alone in bed, bright light piercing his eyeballs as it streamed in from the bedroom's windows, the shades all rolled up. Pots and pans clanged like cymbals downstairs. Jimmy sensed that something was wrong but wasn't up to figuring it out right away.

Why were the shades open? And mother of God, what was Helen doing downstairs?

It wasn't until Jimmy staggered to the bathroom wearing just his tighty-whities, put the seat up, and began to pee that he realized his balls were missing.

Gone. Not even the hint of a scar. But where his two hairy balls were supposed to be... *there was nothing.*

He shrieked, setting off new, bright red alarm bells inside his splitting skull. He stared down in disbelief.

They were gone.

He'd suffered through hangovers before. He'd even begun to wonder recently if perhaps he had a drinking problem. But never, ever, ever had he experienced a hallucination like this. He looked around the bathroom to see what else was wrong. Behind him, the shower with its flowery curtain was pulled closed, as usual. On the other side of the open bathroom door, on the right, was the plain white sink and beside it, the towel rack with its usual three tiers: bath towels on top, facecloths and hand towels on the middle, and extra shampoos, conditioners, tubes of toothpaste and toilet paper on the bottom.

All completely normal. Except for his missing scrotum.

Surely, his eyes could not be trusted. This was simply the mother of all hangovers.

Trying unsuccessfully to calm himself, Jimmy reached *down there*, praying that this was just a visual distortion, not that different from seeing double. Only instead of seeing two where there should be one, he was seeing zero where there should be two.

His hand failed him as surely as his eyes. Beneath his sagging dick—there'd been no "waking up with wood" this morning—hung... *nothing!*

A fresh scream—his—pierced the air. Then a split second later, it pierced his skull.

As if summoned by his agony, Helen appeared just inside the doorframe, a vicious look on her face and fire in her formerly pretty green eyes. She held two frying pans, their bottoms facing each other, poised to mimic cymbals.

"I'd like a Western omelet with a side of bacon, extra crispy, and home fries," she said. "Have it ready in eight minutes."

Jimmy blinked. "I don't cook."

"You do now."

If not for his missing balls, he might have blurted a second instinctive response to follow his first: "But that's your job!" Instead, he spoke the unspeakable.

"Something has happened to my balls!" Jimmy said, his

voice shaking, not believing the humiliating words were escaping his lips. "Or my brain. Or something. I need to get back to bed."

Fury flooded Helen's face. She clanged the two frying pans together twice in succession and then a third time for emphasis. The bathroom echoed with their metallic anger.

"Your balls are mine now," she said. "I've put them away for safekeeping."

Jimmy recoiled. He staggered backward, lightheaded, then before toppling through the curtain and into the shower, he righted himself and staggered back forward until he could steady himself on the back of the toilet. He leaned heavily on it and tried to form words.

"What?" was all he could manage in barely a croak.

Helen nodded. "That's what I said when I got the call last night and heard what you'd done. '*What?*' Pawing a stripper, or something like that, when you were supposed to be playing poker with your dumbass friends? Then getting in a fight with the bouncer because you couldn't bear getting tossed out of the place? You hadn't gotten enough? Hadn't thrown away *all* the money in your wallet to some Trixie or Kandi or Tiffanie?"

Jimmy blinked. Images came flying back into his mind. One gut punch after another. His stomach suddenly felt very queasy.

What had he been thinking?

Of course, he hadn't been thinking at all. Or if he had, it had been with his balls, not his brain.

Jimmy swore softly. "I'm sorry. I—"

Helen crashed the cymbals together with a venom that spared no mercy.

"Not good enough!" she yelled, getting in his face, her eyes all but popping out. "I'm sick of your 'I'm sorry' lame excuses! They mean nothing! So for now and maybe forever, your balls are mine! You will never humiliate me like that again!"

"I'm sorr—"

The frying pans clanged again.

"Western omelet with a side of bacon, extra crispy, and home fries," Helen said. "In eight minutes. Then get down on your knees and scrub this bathroom clean. When you're done with that, mow the damned lawn. It's like a jungle out there. Get the gutters cleaned, then take a shower so you don't smell like a pig because you're taking me out clothes shopping and you'll have to tell me I look wonderful in everything I try on, as wonderful as that stripper you were trying to paw last night, although if you ever bring up her name, I'll put those balls under the car tires and back over them fifty thousand damned times. Got it?"

Wide-eyed, Jimmy nodded.

"Tonight," Helen asked, "would you rather watch chick flicks with me or go with me to the opera?"

The opera? Jimmy thought he'd rather have his eyes gouged out. Besides, the NBA playoffs were tonight. He'd planned to go over Buster's house and drink a thousand beers with the guys and watch the doubleheader.

"Me and the guys were going—" Jimmy began to say, before realizing he was wording it all wrong.

"Play *poker* again?" Helen asked, cocking her head. Her eyes blazed. "Geez, how could I interfere with that!"

"No, the NBA playoffs—"

"They might as well be over," Helen said. "Your balls

are mine. And I'll hear not another word of argument from you."

Jimmy swallowed hard.

"Chick flicks or the opera?" Helen asked.

"Chick flicks. Definitely, chick flicks," Jimmy said.

"Then the opera it is," Helen said, and slammed shut the bathroom door.

***

THE FOLLOWING SATURDAY, Buster showed up at the front door. Almost thirty like Jimmy and the rest of his buddies, Buster was barely five-eight but pushing three bills. Smelling faintly of cheeseburgers and fries, he had unruly, curly black hair and perpetually wore a faded T-shirt, jeans, and sneakers.

"Where you been, Jimmy?" Buster asked. "The guys have all been asking. Every time we text or call you to come out with us, it's always the same answer. 'Sorry. Can't make it.' Even tonight. The seventh game of the series! The seventh game, dude! What's up?"

Jimmy wasn't sure how much he was allowed to divulge. Helen was out shopping or getting her hair done or something. She didn't seem to feel the need to explain anything to him anymore. But even though she was out doing whatever it was she was doing, she'd most certainly brought his balls with her.

She'd made it clear that complaints were no longer allowed, so he kept his big mouth shut. She'd made it clear she would entertain no questions about whether he'd ever get his balls back, so he asked none. But she hadn't made it clear whether or not he could reveal the details of his situation to his buddies. So he tried.

"It's a little embarrassing," Jimmy said, leaning on the doorframe.

Buster frowned. "Dude, can I come in? Grab a beer while you tell me your sad story?"

It was only eleven in the morning, but that had never stopped Buster or the rest of the guys. Or Jimmy, up until this last week, for that matter. They all used the old line that it was five o'clock somewhere.

But it might never again be five o'clock anywhere ever again for Jimmy.

He instinctively stepped aside to let Buster in, then made the first of several shameful admissions.

"Sorry, man, but I ain't got no beer," Jimmy said, averting his eyes.

"You drank it all last night? I thought you was out with your old lady?" Buster said, then apparently remembered the appalling chick flick Jimmy had said he was taking Helen to. "I get it," Buster said. "I'd have needed a case or two after having to sit through that thing."

Jimmy knew better. Helen had said he had drinking problem, a charge hard to refute at this point, and had dumped his remaining supply of Budweisers down the drain.

Down the drain! While he watched!

It had been like watching the execution of a best friend. And not just any execution. A beheading. It would have shriveled up Jimmy's balls. If he still had any.

"Yeah, something like that," he said now, not willing to speak the truth of the demise of his beloved Buds, the term of endearment he'd always used for his Budweisers. *Buds.* Best buds with his Buds. Perhaps another damning piece of evidence that he did have a drinking problem.

Or at least *did* have a drinking problem. Back when he had balls.

As he and Buster turned right into the front room, Buster stopped him, an arm stretched out across Jimmy's chest.

"Whoa!" Buster said with a look of concern usually reserved for those with terminal diseases. "Were you just vacuuming in here?"

The damning evidence, a Hoover upright with matching aqua-colored handle and base, was propped there in plain sight beside the TV and entertainment center that ran along one wall. Up against the opposite wall, dominated by the front picture window, were a matching beige sofa and lounge chair.

Atop the coffee table in front of the sofa was even more damning evidence: the rainbow-colored feather duster Jimmy had also been using to get room looking "spick and span" as Helen had demanded.

Number three on Jimmy's printed list of ten must-do tasks for the day.

"I heard the vacuum running from outside the door," Buster said, "but I assumed it was the dragon lady." He looked all around to make sure they were alone. "But she ain't even here. You were *vacuuming*?"

Jimmy felt his jaw drop but couldn't say a word.

Buster spotted the feather duster, hard to miss with its bright rainbow of colors.

"*And dusting*?" Buster said, horror filling his face. "Jimmy, what has happened to you?"

Jimmy stared at his friend, speechless.

"You've given up drinking and watching sports with your buddies for *vacuuming and dusting the house*?" Buster said. "That's the most pussy-whipped thing I ever heard."

Jimmy couldn't deny the accuracy of the "whipped" part of the equation, but the other half had been nonexistent the last week. Not even close.

He'd hoped that if Helen got in the mood and he got his balls back so he could perform—he wasn't quite sure how that would work but he was hopeful, and surely she couldn't go without sex forever, could she?—then perhaps he'd be allowed to keep them.

But so far, not even a hint. Apparently, having her husband arrested for pawing a stripper, or attempting to paw a stripper or whatever the hell had happened, had sucked Helen bone dry of every last drop of desire.

Not exactly a shocker, Jimmy figured.

"Oh, I got it," Buster said, the light finally dawning. He'd never been the brightest bulb in the chandelier. "Is this all because of what happened at the strip joint?"

Jimmy swallowed hard, still unable to speak. He just nodded sadly.

"How long you gonna be in jail with the dragon lady?" Buster asked.

Jimmy shook his head and shrugged. Then suddenly, the pent up words gushed out.

"She took my balls," Jimmy said, humiliated to have to make the admission but unable to hold the words in any longer. He added, "You can't tell anyone else. Especially not the rest of the guys," even though Jimmy knew for a fact that the rest of the guys would be the *first* ones Buster told. He'd probably text them before he even pulled out of the damned driveway.

Maybe even put it out on twitter.

"Hey, you ain't the first one, you won't be the last," Buster said in his most consoling fashion. "Happens to the best of us."

"No," Jimmy said. "I'm not talking about a figure of speech or a metaphor or whatever the hell it is. I mean literally."

Buster's eyes widened. "Literally? You mean like, *for real?*"

"Yes! God knows when I'll get them back. *If* I ever get them back."

"*Literally?*" Buster asked again, his face all wrinkled up in confused disbelief. "They're gone?"

"Not gone," Jimmy corrected. "In Helen's purse."

"So there's nothing..." A squeamish look came over Buster's face. "There's nothing *down there* anymore?"

"Only my dick. So I can still pee, which is all it's good for now. But Helen has my balls. Both of them."

Buster shook his head and gave a forced chuckle.

"Nice try," he said. "You had me going there for a second."

"I'm serious."

"How stupid do you think I am?" Buster asked, a question that in the past had generated considerable discussion.

"Don't believe me? I'll show you," Jimmy said, unbuttoning his jeans and unzipping the fly.

"Whoa, Jimmy, don't get weird on me," Buster said,

backpedaling so fast he lost his balance and fell backwards on his ass. He crawled back up to his feet with a speed that belied his girth, then with both hands extended, palms out in a keep-away gesture, almost toppled back over again.

"Not that there's anything wrong with that," Buster said, steadying himself on the lounge chair. "I don't care what nobody else does, but... dude, what the hell?"

What the hell, indeed, Jimmy thought. Don't get weird? The last week, his life had been turned worse than weird.

"Trust me, Buster, you ain't my type," Jimmy said. "Not now. Not ever. But until I get my balls back, *no one* is my type."

Buster stared back. Silence hung heavy between them for what felt like forever.

"They're really gone?"

Jimmy nodded sadly.

"And if I needed proof to believe you..." Buster began. "Not that I really want to see, but..." The squeamish look returned to Buster's face, almost as if they were discussing a decomposing body. "I mean, if I just couldn't believe it without seeing it with my own eyes... you could really show me?"

Jimmy nodded.

Buster stood there, now almost fifteen feet away.

"Take a picture," he said. "I'll look the other way, you take the picture with your phone, and show it to me. Or even better, send it to me."

Jimmy shook his head. "I ain't talking no picture of me down there and neither are you or anyone else. That is one dick pic that ain't never happening."

Buster nodded in understanding.

"Okay, I guess I gotta see it," Buster said. "This ain't like showers after gym class or standing at a urinal. I actually gotta see the disgusting thing. Or see what ain't there."

Slowly and filled with shame, as if he was revealing his darkest secret—which was in truth exactly what he was doing—Jimmy lowered his jeans and tighty-whities.

Buster's face went ashen. He staggered drunkenly back and then forward until he grasped the side of the lounge chair and toppled into it.

Though everyone knew he hadn't been to Confession in over a decade, Buster crossed himself and said, "Holy Mother of God."

His eyes stared vacantly at Jimmy. Not at what was missing down there. Eyes to eyes.

Minutes later, as the color finally returned to his face, Buster said, "You gotta get 'em back, Jimmy. You can't live like this. Just take 'em back whether she likes it or not. Don't let the bitch push you around. You're bigger than she is. Be a man, for crying out loud! Just take 'em back. They're yours."

Jimmy wasn't about to point out that without his balls "being a man" was no longer possible. Not only technically. He just didn't think that way—"if you're bigger, take it away"—anymore. His old instincts to fight first, ask questions later—even when the foe was a strip club bouncer capable of putting him in the hospital—didn't exist for Jimmy anymore.

He was a new man. Even if that was just half a man. Or not really a man at all.

And besides the fact that violent instincts no longer

lurked barely below the surface of his mind, Helen had proven that his balls could not be taken back by force.

"She has them tightly wedged into the corner of her purse," Jimmy explained. "She said she'll crush 'em if I try anything funny. Once, by accident—at least I'm pretty sure it was by accident—she dropped the purse, and it felt like the world's strongest soccer player had kicked me hard as hell down there. I was doubled over in agony for almost fifteen minutes."

Buster groaned in pain at the very thought.

Jimmy continued. "She even said if you guys—'your dumbass friends' to quote her directly—try to take them away from her, she'll get away from you somehow and toss the purse underneath the nearest oncoming car. Or if she can't do that, she'll stomp them to bits herself."

Buster groaned again and shook his head. "You sure know how to keep your woman happy."

***

WHEN THE MARITAL icicle known as Helen showed no signs of melting, Jimmy resorted to the kinds of remedies he'd seen on TV.

He began on a Monday with a box of chocolates. Not the expensive stuff. He and Helen had a crushing mortgage, two car payments, and plenty of other large bills, not to mention the ever-present possibility of them having kids in a few years. Her software job appeared secure but there were always rumors of a layoff down at the plant. They had to count every penny.

So Jimmy bought the cheap stuff. After all, it's the thought that counts. Chocolates are chocolates.

When Helen got home from work at close to six-thirty, he was waiting for her just inside the front door. She looked more tired and worn out than usual, but perhaps, he thought, that might make her more receptive. More willing to give in. Too tired to resist anymore.

He thrust the box of chocolates at her, feeling a bit like a first-grader giving his teacher an apple.

"I got these for you," he said, as if a woman smart enough to write software needed an explanation from him. "And the dinner you requested will be out in fifteen minutes. Barbequed chicken, baked potatoes, and corn. You can smell the barbeque now."

Helen appeared suddenly infused with energy. She looked at him as if he was a bug.

"That isn't the dinner I *requested*," she said. "It's the dinner I *demanded*. And if you think a cheap box of chocolates is going to make up for what you did, you're sadly mistaken."

Jimmy blinked. "But we're on a budget. Isn't it the thought that counts?"

"We were on a budget when you were trying to stuff dollar bills into that stripper's G-string," Helen said, eyes blazing. "And the thought counted a hell of a lot when you lied to me about a poker night with the boys that was really a trip to that strip joint. You *lied* to me, Jimmy. What were you thinking about then?"

Jimmy supposed he didn't need to ask for an ETA on when he might get his balls back.

THE NEXT DAY, he waited at the door with a Hallmark card that came with an "I'm sorry" message. As it turned out, he truly was sorry that he'd spent almost ten dollars on nothing more than a damned piece of paper and an envelope.

"That's just another cheap, easy thing that men do to make up for inexcusable behavior," Helen said, flipping the card back at him.

Jimmy wondered what not-so-cheap thing he should try next to make up for his inexcusable behavior. What was his budget? But that didn't seem to be a safe topic. He'd have to take his chances.

So he tried flowers. A dozen long-stemmed red roses. Delivered to Helen's workplace. Cost a fortune. A budget buster to be sure. If Helen still had his balls in her purse when the credit card bill came in, she'd probably toss them under a steamroller or an eighteen-wheeler.

But he had to try.

It didn't work.

Helen breezed by him as Jimmy stood hopefully at the front door. Didn't even look at him.

"You aren't getting your balls back," she said. "Not that cheaply."

"*Cheaply?*" Jimmy said. "Do you know how much those damned roses cost?"

Helen whirled and got in Jimmy's face, so close he could smell her jasmine perfume, powder, and a slight whiff of the day's sweat. Sweet smells on her. Pretty green eyes and long auburn hair. She looked great in her yellow, flowery blouse and tan slacks.

Looked so great he'd be ready to make mad, passionate love to her all night if she could simply return the necessary equipment that was his. He'd take her in his arms and—

She flung his arms away. Arms that he'd tried to wrap around her without even realizing it. Arms that were as repellant to her as weeks-old garbage.

"*Cost?* You want to talk about cost?" Helen asked through gritted teeth. "How about the cost to my dignity to have to drive down to the police station because you got arrested for something like that? You want to talk about cost? A dozen goddamned roses doesn't begin to pay!"

IN THE END, Jimmy did the only thing he could think to do. He tried to win back Helen's heart and trust one day at a time. Not through the quick fixes and band aids of chocolates and flowers or through flowery words written by someone else. And not as a cynical move merely to get his balls back.

He just wanted Helen to be happy again. She deserved it. She deserved better than what he had become. Probably better than he had ever been.

So he would become the person she deserved. Starting with the booze. She'd been right about him having a drinking problem. He'd denied it, but she was right. It was clear to him now.

So Jimmy was finished with alcohol. For good. Not because Helen had dumped all his beer down the drain and he'd been unable, without his balls, to acquire any replacements. No, it was because he did have a problem, and it prevented him from being the person he needed to be.

And if his buddies couldn't be his buddies without him drinking himself blind, then they were no buddies at all. And if they couldn't be his buddies without him being dishonest with Helen and allowing them to call her the dragon lady, then they were no buddies at all.

Jimmy would say good-bye them to all, if need be. They would bust his nonexistent balls and say he'd become someone straight out of the Lifetime channel, but they could all go to hell.

He was going to win Helen back.

None of it would be easy. But it would be worth it.

FOR A TIME, it seemed Helen didn't even notice. Anger still clouded her eyes.

But then one day, she looked at Jimmy anew. The venom dripped away. And Jimmy knew it was time to pour his heart out to her.

He met her at the front door again, this time holding a single rose and his hand over his heart.

"I know I hurt you, and I am so very sorry," Jimmy said. "I can't change what I did, but I will never hurt you like that again. I have changed who I am. I'm trying to be a better person. A person worthy of your love."

Tears pooled in Helen's eyes. Jimmy rejoiced. She had noticed the change in him, after all. Knew these were not idle words.

"I'm not saying this to get my balls back," he quickly added. "What I want to get back most is you. I love you and want to make you happy."

He dropped to one knee. "Will you take me again as your husband, and let me try to make you the happiest woman alive?"

With tears streaming down her face, Helen nodded and reached for her purse.

PERFECTION

INTRODUCTION TO PERFECTION

I wrote "Perfection" for an anthology called *Moonscapes*. I began with the moon's fascinating characteristic of the same side always facing Earth, then combined that with our society's obsession with physical beauty. Many successful stories work that way. They take two fragmentary ideas that by themselves would act as marginally weak launching pads but together form a much more significant story-writing platform. A whole, if you will, that is greater than the sum of its parts.

Perhaps that happened with "Perfection." Perhaps not. I'll let you, kind reader, be the judge.

The story, as it turned out, it didn't quite fit what the *Moonscapes* editor had in mind, but I still loved it. When Leah Cutter decided to run a special science fiction issue in *Mystery, Crime, and Mayhem*, "Perfection" had found its... well, pardon the unintentional pun, but... its *perfect* home.

PERFECTION

The walkways, glistening and spotless, intersected each other at precise ninety degree angles, or at least as precise as those angles could be on the mostly spherical surface of the Moon. Perfect people walked upon the walkways. Every woman featured high cheekbones on her unblemished face, elegant hair of her chosen hue, and the flawless body of a twenty-one-year-old. Every man's chiseled physique was equally young and vibrant without the hint of a wrinkle, receding hairline, or sagging flesh.

The perfect people enjoyed the perfection of their surroundings as was their right, as it had been ever since they'd cleansed the Armstrong Dome of every last bit of ugliness and renamed it appropriately: Perfection.

Tamara and Brett stepped into *Café Magnifique*, savoring their mutual beauty and that of their surroundings, anticipating the pleasure of mouth watering chocolate croissants to go with the café's authentic Cuban coffee. Priceless paintings from Mother Earth hung on the walls: a Carducci, a Thorne, and even an impeccably restored van

Gogh. Nine tables sculpted out of priceless cherry wood were laid out in three widely-spaced rows of three. Tamara and Brett took their accustomed table in the center and nodded their greetings to the other couples, many blue-eyed and golden-haired like Tamara and Brett but none quite their match.

The wait staff, cosmetically pleasing human-like AI's as were all the laborers in Perfection, arrived with their coffees in Sergio Gonzalez cups and saucers and the croissants on matching china.

"What will you do today?" Tamara asked, flashing her flawless smile while placing a hand on Brett's, both hands bearing glittering, jeweled rings on all but their middle fingers and thumbs.

"Perhaps nothing at all," Brett said, returning Tamara's smile with one every bit as radiant. They both understood a day to be an Old Earth day of twenty-four hours and not the Lunar day that was equivalent to almost an Old Earth month. The dome, its diameter just over forty kilometers, provided that illusion even as it provided a transparent view of the black sky above and Earth low on the horizon. The dome provided sixteen hours of light and eight hours of darkness even while the Sun shone for fifteen straight Earth-days and then set, blanketing the lifeless lunar landscape outside the dome in darkness for fifteen more. The dome provided all; it wasn't called Perfection just because of the beautiful people inside.

Brett took his Cuban coffee, sniffed its ambrosia-like, strong scent, then sipped it, enjoying its warming flavor, thinking as always that it was the nectar of the Gods, which of course is what Tamara and he were.

"Let the Earth-bounds and the Discards slave away, as is their fate," he said. "I may do little but drink Magnum Elixir all day and debate philosophy with Malcolm. It is our birthright to do nothing if we so choose, no matter how they may complain."

"Why do you let the Earth-bounds and the Discards concern you?" Tamara asked, her golden hair bouncing as she shook her head. "Their opinion means nothing."

"They concern me not at all, except as fodder for my debates with Malcolm," Brett said, sipping more of the coffee. He and Malcolm, a black man with an impishly iconoclastic bent, had been friends for as long as they could both remember. Brett grinned. "You'll never imagine what he tried to postulate last time."

"What?" Tamara asked.

"That our lives mean nothing more than those of the Earth-bounds." Brett burst into incredulous laughter, prompting amused glances from the other couples, followed a split second later by Tamara. "Can you believe it?"

"Let's look at the poor souls," Tamara said.

"Sure."

Their request registered and the upper half of *Café Magnifique* became transparent, all the way down to the paintings, as was required of all buildings on Perfection.

Tamara and Brett swiveled in their chairs to look upon the beauty of Earth, beautiful now in its full phase for its wispy white clouds and blue oceans, beautiful even more for what the Mother Planet shipped daily to the Moon to keep Perfection in its current state, paid for by the near infinite financial resources of all within.

"I'm sure there are some on Earth who live splendid lives," Tamara. "They can't all be rubes. But our equals?"

Brett shook his head. "Equality is a silly conceit and Malcolm knows it. Our lives by definition mean everything and those on Earth nothing. Why else would we be here and they be there? But Malcolm needs such nonsense to stimulate his intellect. He even began to suggest... you're not going to believe this... he began to suggest that the Discards were also our equals."

"*Discards*?" Tamara exclaimed.

"That argument was beyond even Malcolm," Brett said with a broad grin. "I can't recall the last time we laughed so hard."

"He's a strange man," Tamara said, "although still a feast for the eyes. His strange ideas provide merriment for us all."

"Indeed," Brett said. He bit into the soft, sweet croissant and sipped more of the strong coffee, the cup clinking softly as he set it down on its saucer. "And what will you do today?"

"I thought I might try to see David and Maria," Tamara said, referring to their two perfect children, the boy sixteen years old and the girl fourteen. "It's still premature, but I thought I'd try." The state, of course, was raising them using AI's in the far reaches of the dome. It had done so since taking them from her womb early in the pregnancy before they could impair her appearance, cause her discomfort, or provoke undesirable emotional attachments.

Raising children was a messy business, not fitting for the magnificence of Perfection Proper, an infringement on the ambience. Most became Discards, as had happened only with their first, a child whose name they could now barely recall. *Daniel? Daniella? Nathaniel?* It hardly mattered, what with the unsightly birthmark on its cheek.

"A splendid idea," Brett said.

Tamara flashed her brilliant smile again. "I'm sure they are as beautiful as their genetic perfection dictates."

Brett grinned momentarily before the look of merriment disappeared. A frown formed on his brow. A man with hideously disheveled hair had entered the café and polluted the moment. *Disheveled!* It was an outrage against everything Perfection stood for to allow even a single hair out of its proper place. It sullied the beauty every resident of Perfection had come to require.

"Don't look," Brett said to Tamara, not wishing her day to be as befouled by ugliness as his had just become. Her back was to the door; Brett could spare her this affront. He prepared to trigger the verbal alarm that would summon the AI-cops.

But the first bites of the warm croissant had all but melted in his mouth and the coffee's sharp, strong scent and taste begged for his immediate consumption. Answering the AI-cops' questions would take time. Even allowing for the thermal restoration properties of the matchless Sergio Gonzales china, any delay would compromise his enjoyment. Considering the visual assault that he'd already endured, another affront to his senses would be more than his constitution could be expected to suffer. He'd leave the it to one of the others.

But as Brett looked about, he saw to his dismay that the other couples, engrossed in their fascinating discussions, had all failed to notice the creature. He took another bite of the croissant, savoring the taste. Well, he decided, as long as

The Abomination – no other name did justice to the aesthetic and even psychic trauma it was inflicting on him – as long as it lingered by the doorway, he would wait to sound the alarm until he and Tamara had finished their sumptuous meal. This would follow the Law of Conservation of Beauty, a principle Malcolm had argued in years past and had become part of the accepted canon.

"What is it?" Tamara said with a sly grin, her pale blue eyes riveted on Brett, her back still to the door. "You have a surprise again for me today?"

Brett put his hand on top of hers, felt its sensuous warmth, and was about to say, "Trust me," when *The Abomination* raced toward them, each bounding step lifting well off the floor in the light lunar gravity. Its wild and tangled hair all but floated in the air behind it in hypnotic ugliness.

Too late, Brett stood and triggered the alarm. As Tamara stumbled to her feet, eyes wide, *The Abomination* lunged at her, wielding a knife with a sharp, glistening blade.

Red flashing lights from outside the café exploded into view, making the knife's blade look like it was coated in blood a split second before that became fact. *The Abomination* slashed the knife across Tamara's right cheek and then the left, back and forth, shredding the flesh to ribbons.

"You are worthless!" *The Abomination* hissed, a revolting stream of saliva leaking out of the corner of his mouth. "Your beauty means *nothing*!"

Tamara touched her ruined cheeks and looked at her crimson hand in wide-eyed astonishment. Screams erupted from the other tables where other couples stood riveted for a split second, then broke for the door.

"Worthless!" *The Abomination* shouted, looking all about. "All of you! All of *us*!"

Backing away even as *The Abomination* advanced on him, Brett thought, *You are not one of us! You have never been one of us! No one would—*

Only then did the dawn of recognition flare. *Tyler Chandler? Could it be?* Brett hadn't recognized the old tycoon, one of a long line of Chandler legends. Only weeks ago he'd looked like he was twenty-one, as did they all. But now... now, he'd been reduced to looking like one of Old Earth's proverbial winos: filthy, ugly, and unquestionably deranged.

Chandler slashed his knife through the air, advancing on Brett and missing but coming so close that Brett felt the air whoosh past his face. Particles of Tamara's blood splattered on his skin. Fighting off the revulsion, Brett grasped a cherry wood chair and held it up, warding off Chandler and the swath of his blade.

Two AI-cops burst through the door. Brett froze, hoping Chandler would turn his wrath on them but to no avail. The fiend turned back to Brett and bounded toward him, his eyes beautifully blue and hopelessly insane.

"You, too, Pretty Boy!" Chandler screamed.

But the AI-cops fired their weapons, bringing Chandler down, coating him with a frozen block of an ice-like chemical known well in Perfection. In nanoseconds, it extracted the truth from Chandler, reviewing his life story and ending it without mercy, wrapping a black shroud around him to spare the great and perfect citizens of Perfection from its ugliness any further.

Brett bent over gasping for breath. *That had been a close*

one. He wiped unseemly sweat off his brow and tried to calm his pounding heart.

And then, not wanting to, he looked upon Tamara. He knew he would never again see her flawless face, its skin so soft and smooth. Never again see her radiant smile. The realization filled him with sadness.

At the same time, though, he felt profound relief that he would at least never have to look again on that ruined face in all its irreparable ugliness. For that, Brett was grateful. He would need psychic treatments to wash away the stench of this day, but he would emerge whole.

When the Emergency Response AI's stepped through the door seconds later, Tamara again began to scream, polluting the air with her pain, then turned toward Brett, her arms outstretched.

"This isn't fair! I've done nothing wrong!" Tamara cried.

Brett backed away, feeling his eyes widen in panic, his mouth opening in a silent scream before words emerged. "Keep her away from me!" he commanded and the AI-cops moved in between them.

"I can still be perfect!" Tamara shrieked, tears streaming down her ruined and quite grotesque face.

"Not anymore," Brett said sadly, turning away from her so he would have to view no further ugliness.

"With the treatments, you'd barely be able to tell!" Tamara said.

As the AI's took her away, Brett thought those were the saddest words he'd heard in a long time. As if "barely being able to tell" was good enough for Perfection.

THE EVICTORS, AI's specially designed to pack a Discard's belongings, met Tamara at the airlock. The two of them, a female and a male, loaded her final possessions into the cargo holds of her personalized hovercraft, *The Cleopatra*, and set the auto-pilot for the Pavilion of Peace. A medical AI applied a painkiller to her tattered face so only those unfortunate enough to look upon her would suffer.

"This isn't fair! I'm not a Discard!" she said to the AI's, knowing they would nod sympathetically and then bid her farewell, as they had been programmed to do. Tears streamed down her once lovely but now hideous face, softening the scabs still forming in ugly, ragged lines. She sobbed even though it made her eyes even more red and puffy, giving any viewer of the scene – could she hope that Brett had cared to see her one last time? – no pleasant part of her face to look at.

"Is there no last message?" she begged of the three AI's who looked gravely on. "From Brett?" Knowing she sounded pathetic, adding yet another layer to her new-found ugliness, she added, "From the children?"

The AI's just gave Tamara a sad wave and pointed toward the hovercraft. She looked out onto Perfection, beauty befitting its name for as far as the eye could see, and her heart broke for she would live and breathe there no more.

She stepped inside *The Cleopatra* and sank into the cushioned leather seat anchored at the center of the lush, bejeweled interior. Eight identical seats rimmed the circumference, facing her. The smell of roses filled the cabin. She rested her arms on the armrests, gave the command to open the shades, and watched through the windows that circled the craft as the inner airlock doors closed. Beethoven's "Moonlight Sonata" began to play, the acoustics befitting a concert hall, making the notes of the grand piano so pure and sweet the chords might have been struck a mere handsbreadth away.

Tamara looked at the eight empty seats. *No final words of endearment,* she thought as the craft navigated the multiple airlocks. Of course there had been none from the children. They hardly knew her. They would have only sought to become friends with her at the age of twenty-one when all young people entered polite society looking no younger or older than all those around them.

But no final words from Brett? Nothing like: *Your beauty filled my heart and blessed my life. I will never forget your smile, your laughter, your love. You were beyond compare.*

It was self-indulgent to expect it, she knew. After all, she had sent no kind words of parting when Daniel – or was it Daniella? – had been compassionately discarded. It was better that way, everyone knew that. A clean break. But Tamara had known self-indulgence all her life, had reveled in it, in fact, and it was hard not to expect it now.

She wondered how Daniel, or Daniella, looked. How old would he or she be? Tamara grimaced. Did she really care? The birthmark would no doubt be hideous by now, perhaps even as large as a fingernail.

The Cleopatra glided along the barren moonscape, the sky black in the lunar night, until the Mountain of Peace came into view. It was no mountain, not yet, barely even a hill rising out of the flat plain of *Mare Imbrium* in which

Perfection was centered, but it was significant for what it represented.

The Cleopatra swung wide around the mountain, coming no closer than the half-kilometer limit, and continued on auto-pilot to the Pavilion of Peace, a dome with a diameter of little more than three hundred meters. The hovercraft entered the double-airlock system, and in short order Tamara stepped into the pavilion.

The foyer, though modest in size with low ceilings and an area barely larger than that of *Café Magnifique,* almost rivaled Perfection in its opulence. The marble floors echoed with Tamara's soft, lunar-gravity footfalls. The walls, made of imported mahogany and cedar, filled the air with their pleasing, ancient scent. From behind a door in the far wall, an AI sculpted to look like the Old Earth actor Clark Gable rushed to her side.

"May I get you a drink, Tamara?" he asked. "We have an exquisite Burgundy of the finest vintage. Imported from France, of course, and stored in our climate-controlled cellars. Or perhaps you'd like something stronger? Or something to eat?"

Tamara touched her scarred face, noticing that Gable's eyes never left her own. He didn't recoil from her in disgust the way that Brett had or the handful of onlookers that had filled *Café Magnifique.* But the handsome man was just an AI, his failure to be repulsed a mere matter of programming.

"I'll take the Burgundy," she said, "but be prepared to fill my glass many times."

Gable smiled. "Of course. It's on its way." He pointed her to the far wall from which he'd emerged. "Come with me," he said, and guided her into a small, darkened theatre. "Take a seat," he said, pointing to the five rows of five seats each. "Can I bring you anything else?"

Tamara shook her head. She took the center seat of the center row and sank into the plush leather. Gable returned, bowed, and handed her the wine. She examined the glass, a Waterford Crystal, then swirled the Burgundy and sniffed it. A premium vintage indeed. She sipped it, letting the wine wash over all her taste buds.

"Exquisite as you promised," Tamara said with a smile. The smile wasn't for Gable, a mere bucket of bolts, after all, even though he was a dreadfully handsome one, but rather for herself. She could enjoy at least this pleasure before she was done. She sipped more wine, and its warmth emanated from her belly. She felt better still. Gable rushed to her side and refilled the glass.

"I'll leave you now, and grant you your privacy," he said. "If you'd care for more wine or need me in any way, just wave your hand. Sensors will inform me and I'll be here in an instant."

Tamara nodded and sipped the Burgundy. All things considered, she was feeling very good.

Total darkness fell inside the theatre and a deep voice boomed from all around her. *Welcome, Tamara.*

The ceiling and lower walls became transparent as if opening up to the black sky of the lunar night. Low on the horizon hung the blue-and-white, near-full globe of Mother Earth, the most beautiful treasure in the heavens. In the foreground, slightly off-center, stood the great dome Perfection.

You face an important decision, the deep voice said. *You have the right to continue on to the Dome of Discards, where on the Far Side which never sees Mother Earth, you will face more ugliness than you can bear.* Her chair swiveled 180 degrees. Upon the wall, images of rats climbing over each other filled the screen. *Possible overcrowding. Abominations like none you have ever seen.*

The rats turned into humans – revolting humans with misshapen faces that bore appallingly low cheekbones, scars, and birthmarks. A woman with a harelip came into full view and stepped closer and closer. Tamara shrieked and shrunk back into her chair, realizing only on a distant, subconscious level that she had spilled the wine. She tried to get away from the hideous woman who kept coming closer and closer. Then next to the harelipped woman, a young Latin man with a terribly scarred face and mismatched eyes gazed upon Tamara and smiled. The vermin of the human race climbed all over each other and drew closer and closer still.

"Stop!" Tamara screamed.

The images faded to black. Slowly, her chair swiveled back to face Mother Earth. Tamara trembled at the horrors she'd just seen and drew in short, quick gasps of air. It smelled faintly metallic, not at all like the pleasing scents of mahogany and cedar outside in the foyer or the varied sensual fragrances of Perfection's air.

The Far Side is not a place for beautiful people, the voice said. *And you were among the most beautiful of all. You inhaled the beauty of Perfection and you exhaled it in kind, a treat for every inhabitant.*

Gable rushed up to Tamara and filled her glass, steadying her shaking hand so she could drink.

You may go on to the Dome of Discards, the deep voice continued. The transparent ceiling and upper walls clouded, then turned to black, cutting off the view of the blue-and-white globe and Perfection below it. *If you do, then in death, as in the rest of your life, you will not see Mother Earth. Your ashes will remain on the Far Side, on The Mountain of Sorrow, where they will be mixed in with the ashes of all manner of horrors. Discards. The diseased. Criminals such as the one who attacked you.*

The hideous woman with the harelip returned in full view on the wall, then exploded into flames. Ashes rained down upon Tamara, who put her arms across her face, jostling the wine while trying to shield herself from this indignity.

Or you can remain on the Near Side and remain with those of your kind, the voice said, suddenly soothing and inviting. *You can take your rightful place on the Mountain of Peace, spending eternity looking out on Mother Earth and the great dome of Perfection, all in perfect alignment, your ashes mingling with those from Perfection who have gone on before you and those who will follow.*

For though you have been scarred, you are genetically perfect, and so you can join the Mosaic of the Beautiful that every year rises higher and higher above the otherwise barren moonscape, your contribution adding four percent of your original body mass as the mountain reaches into the heavens with its beauty, surpassing the drab ugliness of all around it.

Already, the Mountain of Peace is visible from Earth when viewed through powerful telescopes. Many look upon it from Perfection. Beauty deserves to be on display; ugliness must be banished to the Far Side where no man, woman, or beast must see it.

The decision is yours to make. For a split second, the theatre fell silent. *But is there really a choice?*

TAMARA KNEW she'd never subject herself to the Dome of Discards. The very thought made her skin crawl. And to be subjected to an eternity on the genetic slagheap known as the Mountain of Sorrow, forever looking out on the barren moonscape commingled with the dregs of society, would be unspeakable.

She would, of course, consent to her humane cremation and take her place proudly atop the ever-rising Mountain of Peace.

But she couldn't help thinking it was all so premature. Wouldn't it be a tragedy for a beauty of her stature to be extinguished before its time and thereby be denied to the people of Perfection? They had gloried in her splendor for so many years. Her genetic perfection was such that she had created two flawless offspring and only a single Discard, while most produced a dozen or more wretched things that had to be quickly flushed to the Dome of Discards. The place would be teaming with all of them.

Considering her surpassing greatness, she owed it to the people of Perfection, if not herself, to present herself at the gates of the city and make one last attempt to persuade those who had drank so fully of her beauty that they could still drink again and again. Surgeries easily performed by the medical AI's could restore almost all of that which they'd loved. For someone such as herself, surely 99.99 percent of perfection was greater than 100 percent of her inferiors, all beautiful people, but none a match for her.

She could become a legend. Tamara the Great, the first to suffer an unsightly attack only to overcome it with her otherwise surpassing beauty. When she eventually took her place on the Mountain of Peace, they would compose songs about her, immortalizing her above all others.

And so Tamara – not yet Tamara the Great, but soon to become so, she was sure – raced out of theater and bounded toward the airlock where *The Cleopatra* waited.

"Tamara," Gable said, a note of rising alarm in his voice. "You haven't authorized your Final Request."

Tamara ignored him. He was, after all, just an AI.

"You're making a huge mistake!" Gable said, horror written all over his face.

She stepped inside the inner airlock and pressed the button on the wall to shut its door. Without looking back, she followed into the outer airlock, entered *The Cleopatra*, and took her place in the center seat. She issued the commands to close the hatch, close the blinds, and depart as soon as the airlock system gave its approval.

She set the auto-pilot for Perfection and programmed it to wake her as soon as she was five minutes away. She'd suffered a day like none other. A nap would refresh her and give her that extra sparkle she was known for.

Tamara the Great, she thought as she reclined her chair and drifted off, smiling. It had a nice ring to it.

SHE AWOKE to the sound of Beethoven's Fifth Piano Concerto, the gorgeous Adagio second movement, her requested wake-up music. Its beauty always inspired her.

Yawning, she sat up. The nap had been a stroke of genius. She felt *so* well-rested she was ready to jump out of her skin. She would wow them, one and all.

Tamara ordered the system to keep the blinds closed. She wouldn't announce her presence ahead of time. She'd use the element of surprise and let whoever was waiting think it was only an AI returning the hovercraft for asset dispersal purposes.

Tamara felt *The Cleopatra* gently enter the outer airlock on auto-pilot and set down. She opened the blinds, saw the airlock flashing green, signifying it was safe to exit, and after confirming her safety with *The Cleopatra's* sensors, she gave the command to open the hatch and stepped out. Tamara continued into the inner airlock, the words she would use to persuade whoever waited on the other side echoing through her head.

Would a rose one petal plucked, still not smell so sweet?

It sounded Shakespearian. How could that fail to convince? Tamara pressed the button to open the inner airlock door and froze.

An empty dome stretched out before her for as far as the eye could see. Lifeless. Tomb-like. There was... *nothing*.

No people.

No AI's.

Not even buildings.

The dome was dead, its air stale and metallic.

Tamara spun around. The double-airlock system with the hovercraft parked in the outside airlock looked like

Perfection's, but it also looked like every other double-airlock she'd ever seen.

But this sure wasn't Perfection. And it wasn't the Pavilion of Peace. What other lunar domes were there?

Panic welled up inside her. This couldn't be... it just couldn't be the Dome of Discards. If it were, it would be teeming with monstrosities. Tamara reeled as the image of the rats crawling all over each other flashed into her mind.

No, this was someplace quite different. But what could it be? Had her command to return to Perfection been over-ridden? It must have been. Or had she been turned away from Perfection and then sent here on auto-pilot.

But where was *here*?

She stepped inside. The empty dome reverberated with every footfall. No marks on the curving metallic walls surrendered a clue to its identity.

Tamara navigated through the airlocks back to *The Cleopatra*. She queried the sensors and stared at the result.

This was the Dome of Discards. The positional readout didn't lie. A shiver ran down her back.

But how could it be so empty? There was *nothing* here. Where was Daniel, or Daniella, or whatever its name was? Where were all the other Discards?

Hadn't the booming, deep voice back at the Pavilion of Peace spoken of overcrowding, like the rats crawling all over each other? That's what she'd expected. Perfection's Discards had been sent in countless numbers to live here. It was only her impeccable genetic heritage that had limited her and Brett to just one.

Tamara made her way back inside and stared at the

empty dome. It defied comprehension. And then, as if to offer her an answer, the dome became transparent.

Tamara opened her mouth in a silent scream.

Not because the Sun was high in the sky and Earth nowhere to be seen. She had expected that much here on the Far Side. No, it was something far worse.

Outside, the Mountain of Sorrow rose into the lunar sky, unspeakably high, so much grander in scale in its deformity than the Mountain of Peace, towering by comparison.

It can't be, Tamara thought. *So high!*

Tamara looked at the empty dome. *All* of the Discards. *Daniel. Daniella.*

Eyes wide in horror, Tamara ran for *The Cleopatra*.

Get out of here! she screamed to herself. *Get out!*

She got as far as the first airlock.

Thank you for your sacrifice, a deep, booming voice echoed as she stood trapped between the airlock doors.

A familiar voice.

"No!" Tamara shouted. "You said—"

The gas, green and swirling and acidic, poured into the airlock, choking off Tamara's words.

The Mountain of Sorrow, the deep voice said in a tone of proud satisfaction, *grows every day.*

THE SHORT LIFE AND HORNY TIMES OF A TEENAGE MANTIS

INTRODUCTION TO THE SHORT LIFE AND HORNY TIMES OF A TEENAGE MANTIS

This story came out of the opportunity to contribute to an anthology loosely themed "Non-human." I wrote what I thought was a funny, if not outright hilarious, story. The editor, who had previously bought several of my stories and I therefore considered a receptive audience, was not amused.

Not... a... fan. At least not of this story. Oops.

That's how it goes when you take chances. If you always play it safe and write straight down the middle, you offend no one but run the very real risk of boring everyone.

I write stories that sometimes leave readers shaking their heads, questioning my sanity. (See, for example, "The Birth of Booger Nation.") Other readers might react a bit more gently and merely feel a story of mine is "too far out there" or simply not to their taste.

I can live with all of the above. As long as my stories aren't boring.

No one has called "The Short Life and Horny Times of a Teenage Mantis" boring.

As you may have gathered from these introductions, Dean Wesley Smith is a kindred twisted spirit. He bought the story for *Pulphouse Fiction Magazine*, Issue 18, then chose it again to lead off *Implode the Membrane: Stories from Pulphouse*. In both introductions, he said, "This might be one of the most perfect *Pulphouse* stories I have read in a long time."

THE SHORT LIFE AND HORNY
TIMES OF A TEENAGE MANTIS

It's love at first sight.

Or at least heart-pounding, wing-flapping, propagate-the-species-and-I-mean-now-baby-*now* animal lust. Insect lust, which even the dumbest primate knows is the best kind, the reason we're going to swarm over the entire world some day. Cover every last inch with our hard exoskeletons, our three pairs of legs, and our clicking mandibles. More specifically, I'm feeling praying mantis lust, the most supreme and powerful of all lusts.

Green means go, baby.

That's what I feel the first time I see Raptrix, the hot new praying mantis in our corner of the verdant jungle. I'm hanging on a ripe green stem on the outside of a thick cluster of ferns, head pointed diagonally toward the sky, waiting for my next meal to arrive – a juicy fly, bee, or butterfly perhaps – when I spot her out of the corner of my compound eyes.

She's fifteen feet away down on the ground below, crouching on a bed of ragged green leaves next to a tangle of tall leafy bushes. She's hard to make out at first, her luscious green body sadly camouflaged by the leaves and all the other surrounding greenery. High above, the thick, leafy canopy of a tree blocks out the sunlight down here below, cloaking her in a dark shadow most unbefitting a creature of her beauty.

To get a better look, I turn my head around to face her directly, rotating it one hundred and eighty degrees as all mantises can do, yet another example of our supremacy over other insects and certainly over the stiff-necked, soft, foul-smelling primates.

A beauty, she is.

The heavens open as a beam of light breaks through the leafy canopy above and Raptrix is suddenly bathed in the spotlight she deserves. Her head is perfectly triangular, every bit as exquisite as the rounded heads of primates are formless and ugly. It swivels on her long sensuous neck that turns about to survey her surroundings. I can only hope she will see me with those lovely green bulbous compound eyes and their tiny dark spot at the center. *The better to see me with, oh darling*. Her mandibles will drop in astonishment and her beaklike snout will quiver with desire.

For me. Though I am small even for a male, little more than half the length of a human's finger compared to a female's near full length and broader thorax and abdomen, I am big where it counts.

In my heart.

It beats passionately for Raptrix and Raptrix alone. Is there a finer creature in the universe than her? I gasp at the way her antennae sway sensuously this way and that. It is as if they are beckoning me to come mate with her right now.

There will always be food to catch, my love, she seems to say. *Come to me. Take me, now. Mount me, you big hunk of mantis!*

Hubba hubba.

What if she were to use her wings, the outer set narrow and leathery, the hind ones oh so delicate, to fly to me and let me pour my passion out all over her? Or should I fly to her?

No, it is not yet time. I am not yet ready.

Oh, I am ready, *ready, ready!* for the mounting. The green stem of a fern I cling to quivers with my passion. But a beauty such as her has many suitors, of which I will be just one. I must think of what I will say, the magic words to capture her heart. Better yet, I will bring her a gift. A fat, juicy fly, the tastiest delicacy in the jungle. If only one will alight nearby, I will pounce on it, seize it, and forgo devouring it myself even though hunger roars inside me. I will bring it to Raptrix and watch her matchless mandibles bite off its head. Some of its juices might drip off her triangular head, but I am sure she will waste little. She will consume the whole thing, and then, filled with gratitude and an irresistible attraction for the hunter who has brought her such a fine treat, she will look more favorably upon me than all others. Though my rivals may be larger than I am, I will be the one who wins her heart.

But alas, no fly, bee, or butterfly alights nearby. I have no gift to bring my beloved. For now, I must only look upon those spiked forelegs with desire. I covet that deliciously plump, rounded abdomen.

I'm a thorax fan, myself. I like 'em hard and bright and shiny green. But Raptrix surely has the plumpest, roundest abdomen I have ever seen. Voluptuous. Oh, the thought of mounting it, feeling its perfect smoothness beneath me, the tips of my tarsus caressing its curves, and then plunging my kusik—

"What're you looking at?" asks a sneering voice beside me, making me almost fall off my perch upon the fern.

It is Manto, my best friend, hanging on a nearby fern stem, a smirk splashed across his mandibles. He begins to laugh, a raspy, coarse laughter that sounds as if he's rubbing the jagged ridges of his coxa, high on his legs, together.

"Nothing," I say sheepishly and adjust my position on the ripe green stem where I have been patiently awaiting my prey. It's best not to move so my own green coloration camouflages me from my next meal, which won't know I'm there until it's too late. Movement is my enemy. But Manto has rattled me and besides, my current position has provided me no opportunities. I can only do better else-where on the stem. A little closer to the ground, perhaps. In better position to snare my prey.

And closer to Raptrix.

"She's something, isn't she?" Manto says.

"Who?" I ask, flustered. I scurry even closer to the ground.

"Who do you think?" Manto asks. He's larger than I am – though who isn't? – but he's certainly no freak, no rival in size for a female. His full length reaches only to the top of a female's neck, and the breadth of his thorax and abdomen are no match for hers. His greenish hue is the tiniest bit darker than my own, as is the pigmentation in his compound eyes. His mandibles always seem to be set in a mocking angle.

"Come on, I'm your best friend," he says. "You can be honest with me. I saw you ogling Raptrix. For a second there, I almost thought you were doing that primate thing. You know, the thing that makes them go blind?" His mandibles chitter in laughter.

I want to fly over to him and bite off his head. Rip it off and devour every last crunchy part. How dare he tarnish my love for Raptrix with so much as the thought of such a foul primate act?

We are praying mantises. Our mating is passionate but pure. We are not chimpanzees or humans. We are a dignified species. Were we not created to rest in a praying posture, as if constantly thanking our Creator that we are not primates? Fouling our language with the disgusting practices of humans and chimps is beneath us. Manto should be ashamed of himself.

But of course I don't fly to him and bite off his head. I utter no complaint. When you're the runt of the litter, you're in no position to command your will.

I will show him, however. When Raptrix submits to my charms – to my love – and I mount that lovely, plump abdomen and inject the seed that will spawn our next generation, I will get the last laugh. It will be my descendants that populate the Earth, not Manto's or any of the other males who mock me because of my size.

"I don't blame you, Ralphie boy," Manto says. "I don't blame you one bit."

Yes, my name is Ralph. A terrible name for a praying mantis, a burden I have borne from birth. According to tradition, the runt of a litter is given a human name. Apologists for this appalling tradition say it exists to make the smallest mantis feel larger, but we all know better. There can be no good being associated with primates. In truth, it is nothing but an additional insult packed on top of the indignity of my lack of size. My name doesn't make me feel larger; it reminds me, and every other mantis, that I am less than them all.

I am the least of those among me.

Ralph. Ralphie. I spit the name out, and though there is nothing I can do to stop others, I refuse to utter it myself. There is not one human-like thing about me! Yes, I am small, I admit it. But I am not a foul, ugly human, pardon the redundancy.

"I'm gonna take a shot at her myself," Manto says, tearing me harshly away from my self-loathing reveries. "She's one hot number!"

The words chill me. Manto, my best friend. With my beloved.

"What a sweet, plump abdomen!" he continues. "Whooo-eee! Climb aboard and hold on for dear life! What a ride! She's the Creator's gift to my kusik."

My insides roil. But why should I be surprised? I know I have rivals. Every male mantis in flying distance is my rival. They all will be courting Raptrix. Why should Manto be any different?

And what chance does that leave me, the runt of the litter?

"You're talking like a primate," I say. "Have some respect for yourself. You're a praying mantis, the highest of all species. Act like it! Show some dignity."

"Have I said anything you haven't already thought?"

Not in exactly the same words, I admit, though only to

myself. My thoughts have been filled with passion, but they have been imbued with love and adoration. And besides, it's different saying the words aloud so brashly. Passion propagates the species. Without it we will all die. But must we reduce ourselves to speaking of it like the humans?

"I share your attraction," I say, "but not the barbarity with which you express it."

"Raptrix will appreciate *all* of the barbarity with which I express it," Manto says, thrusting his lower body forward as if he's mating with the fern stem upon which he hangs. His mandibles click with glee. "Oooo-eeee! I might come close to shattering that abdomen with my enthusiasm."

WHEN THE TIME COMES, her abdomen does not, of course, shatter. And of course, it is Manto who gets the opportunity to mate and not me.

Why I ever thought Raptrix would mate with me is a question for which I have no answer. It can only be explained by the depth of my love, and admittedly my lust, for her and how it clouded my mind to the harsh truth of my stature. Runts of a litter inevitably die as frustrated virgins. Nature has no wish for future generations of me.

Manto's chance comes days after we first spot her, but days are a long time for a mantis. Manto and I are both only several months old, but that's eighteen in mantis years. And so it is that Manto says to me as we hang on our accustomed ferns, "I know you've had your eyes on Raptrix, but time is a wastin', my friend. Besides, a hot number like her needs a studly mantis like me. Raptrix needs to listen to some Manto music. She needs a heaping portion of Manto romance. She needs a powerful injection of some Manto juice."

I hate it when he refers to himself in the third person, but that pales in comparison to how I feel about what he's just said and what he's about to do. But most of all, I hate what he says next.

"No offense, Ralphie boy, but a pale green runt like you just isn't up to the challenge of a mantis like Raptrix," he says. "If you were, you'd have mounted that hot mama a long time ago. She needs a stud like me. Watch, Ralphie boy, and see how it's done. When I'm done with her, you're gonna see one mantis mama with a big smile on her mandibles."

And so I watch with heartbroken fascination as he scuttles down the fern stem and approaches Raptrix. She's crouching now in a patch of thick green grass, motionless, waiting for a grasshopper or cricket to jump into her deadly grasp or close enough for her to pounce.

"Hey, baby," Manto says, his antennae swinging wildly atop his head.

Hey, baby? That's the best introductory line Manto could come up with? *Hey, baby?* If there's a praying mantis that deserves a human name, it's Manto, not me. *Hey, baby?*

But Raptrix doesn't turn him away. He takes a step closer, and I see a smile creep across her mandibles. My beloved is falling for his crude advances. She showers him with the indescribable smells of her love. I catch a whiff of the scent and it stabs at my heart because I know it isn't meant for me.

I turn away and shut off my hearing. I can't bear to

watch or listen. I'd shut off my sense of smell, too, if I could. It should be me creeping up to her, not Manto. Not my best friend wooing her – successfully! – with *Hey, baby*!

I look the other way and try to think of something else, anything else, but in no time, my eyes are drawn back to the couple, my Raptrix and Manto.

He's crawling atop her. His forelegs wrap themselves around her lovely green thorax.

It feels as though the thousands of lenses in my compound eyes are about to pop out and shatter. But stunningly not from revulsion.

As Manto presses himself against Raptrix's wonderfully plump and rounded abdomen, I learn something appalling about myself.

I like to watch.

Does that make me sick? Perverted? Perhaps, but I watch Manto and my beloved Raptrix, feeling no guilt or even jealousy, only a vicarious thrill that borders on ecstasy.

With his forelegs wrapped around her lovely green thorax and his thin lower body pressed against Raptrix's sublime, plump abdomen, Manto extends his kusik. It looks like a fat, green, engorged caterpillar, snaking around to the underside of her abdomen.

The tip of it probes her. Touching. Searching.

And then it finds its mark.

It plunges in.

Manto's kusik spasms, over and over.

The two of them thrash about, locked together, in the midst of the grasses. I think for only the briefest moment that it should be me coupling with my beloved and not my crude friend, but I push that thought away. I don't want to sully the moment, reduce the pleasure I feel at their carnal embrace.

This is enough.

Their grappling becomes even more feverish. Manto's kusik continues to spasm. Over and over. Unlike the pathetically swift mating of the primates, this will, I know, continue for hours.

And I will watch it all. Thrilling at the sight.

Raptrix swivels her head about to face him. Since his length only reaches to her neck, she cranes downward and her bulbous eyes gaze into his. For the briefest instant I feel a pang of jealousy. Clearly, she feels such longing for my friend that she must lock eyes with him as they continue their union, their mutual bliss. She feels a special bond with Manto, who could muster no better than a "Hey, baby" come-on.

Why not me?

I can't help ask myself the question, even though I know that as a runt, I have no right to dream that this most beautiful of mantises would ever even give me a second glance. That is my answer, even though I can't help ask the question yet again – *why not me?* – as I see their eyes lock onto each other and Manto's kusik spasms its juices into Raptrix's abdomen.

And then... and then...

Raptrix leans close to Manto until their mandibles almost touch.

And she bites off half of his head!

I can't believe my eyes. I recoil, my lower mandible dropping in astonishment. I almost fall off my perch on the fern stem. Raptrix bit off half of Manto's head!

And now… now she bites off the other half!

Manto keeps right on going. If anything, his kusik spasms even more feverishly. So, too, does Raptrix keep on, consuming my headless friend bite by bite until her flexible, articulating neck can extend no farther downward, her voracious mandibles can strain and reach no lower part of Manto's body to feast without detaching herself from his quivering kusik.

She waits patiently for it to complete its task, and when it does and the headless husk of his body finally topples lifelessly to the ground, Raptrix devours every last morsel of my friend, leaving behind little more than an empty green shell. With her mouth, she cleans off the tips of her tarsus, sure not to waste any of him.

I watch it all in horror and growing fascination. Spellbound by the images replaying in my mind of Manto's headless body copulating with Raptrix, his kusik spasming with even more feverish enthusiasm after his demise, I wonder if his performance improved because he was no longer encumbered by the burden of conscious thought. This was, after all, a mantis who, friend or not, could manage no better than, "Hey, baby," as his opportunity to extend himself to the next generation.

Am I being unfair? Perhaps. But we runts of the world suffer many indignities, some even at the hands of friends like Manto. We can't always cover ourselves in goodness, sacrifice, and deference. Not when our greatest thrills are the vicarious enjoyments we experience through others. Sometimes, the least of us must speak the harsh truth, even about our friends. And sometimes, the least of us wonder if we can actually achieve more than just the vicarious thrill. Maybe we can have it all.

Which is why the thought returns to me, as insane now as it was understandable before.

Why not me?

I APPROACH Raptrix with my offering of love, a grasshopper firmly clasped in my spiked forelegs, still alive and wriggling in my grasp. A carcass is, of course, no gift for a queen. She descends the green leafy bush from where she was perched and approaches along the grassy jungle floor. Before she nears striking range, I bite off the crunchy head of the grasshopper, lay it down, and back away.

I am no fool. Or at least my foolishness has its limits.

"For you, my queen," I say.

She pounces on the still-warm meal, and I listen to her mandibles clack as I move behind her. I slip onto her back, my head reaching only to the middle of her exquisite thorax as my slender abdomen presses against the plump curvature of hers, sending a shiver of excitement through my entire being.

This is the key moment. If she will not have me, she will stop me now and I will have to flee for my life lest I find that I have brought her two meals, not one, the grasshopper and myself. And indeed, I know that outcome could also be true even if she accepts me. In fact, it may even be more likely if that's the case. The nearby husk of Manto's body is proof of that.

Instead, Raptrix continues to feast greedily on the

grasshopper. And so I caress the thorax of my dreams with my forelegs, and in my mind speak of my love for Raptrix. I dare not speak it aloud and distract her, but my thoughts speak volumes.

You are the fairest, my dear, the loveliest mantis in all the land, nay, in all of creation. I have loved you from the moment I saw you and I have loved or lusted for no other. Please be mine.

Since my triangular head reaches only to the middle of her thorax, I brush the tips of my mandibles against her hard green shell, and with the scent of love in the air, extend my kusik. It snakes around to her underside, probes, and almost instantly finds its home.

I thrust my kusik in.

Ooo-baby. Ooo-baby. Ooo-baby.

With joyous enthusiasm, I plunge it deeper into Raptrix. *Oh, love of my life. My beauty. My queen. We are united. We are one.*

My forelegs grasp hold of Raptrix's lower thorax. My kusik spasms triumphantly. The fluid of my love enters her.

Ooo-baby. Ooo-baby.

I thank my Creator that I am no mere primate. I will enjoy this bliss for hours. Bask in it. Rejoice in it.

Ooo-baby. Ooo-baby.

Raptrix, you are my beloved. My one and only.

As if summoned, she swivels her neck around to look at me. It cranes downward, and I gaze with love into her green eyes, the tiny, dark spot in their centers focused on me.

I am her beloved, as she is mine.

Ooo-baby. Ooo-baby.

Her triangular head darts forward and her mandibles open wide.

But they snap shut just short of me. I feel the whoosh of air wash over my head. I feel my kusik spasm even more feverishly.

Raptrix stares at me in astonishment. Again, she lunges at me, but my spiked forelegs hold tight to the base of her thorax, and though she strains to reach me, she cannot. There are limits to the flexibility of even her articulating neck.

Again and again, her mandibles snap at me, but fall short and bite into nothing but air.

Ooo-baby. Ooo-baby.

For the first time in my short life, I thank my Creator that I am a runt.

Is that a radiant glow about Raptrix this morning? It's hard to describe exactly, but in the bright sunlight poking through the trees above to where she clings to a branch on a small, thick bush, her green thorax and abdomen sparkle in a way I've never seen before.

Can it be that I satisfied my love's every desire last night and she basks today in that lingering satisfaction, as I still glow in mine?

What else can it be? Can there be any doubt that we are meant for each other?

I will admit that after our lovemaking was over last night I barely escaped her clutches. I almost became her second meal. But I was quick, a second blessing to being small. And I am sure she attempted to devour me only out of reflex. As she becomes accustomed to our love and the satisfactions of our passions, I am sure she will first suppress and then totally disavow herself of that base instinct. After the consummation of our love, we will bask in its glow.

Together. Always.

And so I scurry down the stem of my fern to the bed of leaves below where Raptrix, my beloved, my most wondrous lover, awaits.

I am sure that today, and every future day with her, will be even better than the day before.

TWO-MINUTE DRILL

INTRODUCTION TO TWO-MINUTE DRILL

I wrote this story for an anthology with a theme of alien invasions in the recent past. So did Contrarian David H. Hendrickson focus on bug-eyed monsters in their gleaming spaceships with faster-than-light drives?

By now you know the answer.

"Two-Minute Drill" instead opens in 1980 with three Texas good old boys in a doublewide drinking Lone Star beer while watching Howard Cosell and Dandy Don Meredith on Monday Night Football.

My kind of story.

It was a ton of fun to write and all five professional editors who read it at a workshop I was attending loved it. Traditional publishing, however, was collapsing (again) at the time and indie publishing had not yet gotten a foothold. As a result, the alien invasion anthology never saw the light of day.

Years later, though, "Two-Minute Drill" was a perfect fit for the wonderfully titled anthology *Snot-Nosed Aliens*.

TWO-MINUTE DRILL

December 15, 1980
Dallas, Texas

So we was watching that old blowhard Howard Cosell and Dandy Don Meredith on Monday Night Football. There was that other guy in the broadcast booth, Frank Gifford, but we didn't much pay him no mind even though he did the play-by-play. The windbag and Dandy Don was the show and everyone knew it.

We was watching in my doublewide, sitting on my sagging, food- and beer-stained couch, a broken spring goosing Fat Freddie or Jimmy Lee every five minutes so them cranky sumbitches had something to complain about besides the damned Cowboys, who was getting goosed pretty good themselves by the Los Angeles Rams, 21-0. I was about the only one not getting no goosing on account of me sitting on the sofa's good end that was right snug up against the wall with the Velvet Elvis. Hey, it's my doublewide and my sofa, even if it's all an ugly piece of shit with no elbow room. It was also my Lone Star Beer them freeloaders was drinking, empty cans littering the gray carpet that once was new but now has so many dark stains they look like drunken polka dots.

Three empty pizza boxes sat sloppily stacked beside Fat Freddie's end of the sofa. We'd emptied them suckers out by the end of the first quarter, but I could still smell the pepperoni and taste the peppers and onions. While the Rams huddled, we all puffed on our Marlboros, adding to the thick blue cloud of cigarette smoke hanging in the air. Fat Freddie added something extra, lifting one prodigious cheek and letting rip. So much for smelling the pepperoni.

On the TV that was not even a first down away from where we sat, Vince Ferragamo completed another pass. The Rams was kicking the Cowboys all over the damned field.

Jimmy Lee rubbed his close-cropped scalp, then scratched his scraggly beard. "If this don't get no better, I'm callin' it a night after halftime," he said. "After Cosell." Howard Cosell narrated highlights of Sunday's games and none of us ever missed it, not even to empty bladders that felt close to exploding. Even if the sumbitch was a pompous windbag, you had to love the way he said on touchdowns, "He... could... go... all... the... way." I swear, when I had Bobby Sue in the back seat of my crew cab pickup a couple weekends ago, I was hearing Howard saying those same words about me. Course, I never did get in the end zone.

Jewerl Thomas, a rookie for the Rams who was making our linebackers look like girly-men, ran off tackle for six yards.

"Jimmy Lee," I said. "You can leave if you want, but I don't turn this set off until Dandy Don sings 'The party's over.' House rule. Hell, it's the one time that Howard shuts up."

"What are you talking 'bout, Clete?" Jimmy Lee said. "Howard don't shut up even then."

Jimmy Lee might have had me on that one.

"Can't believe I had to hear about John Lennon last week from that gasbag," Fat Freddie said, his jowls jiggling as he shook his head. The color in his cheeks drained, and his lips turned unnaturally pale.

Silence, broken only by Frank Gifford's play-by-play, hung in the air as somber as the cloud of cigarette smoke was thick. We'd all been fourteen or fifteen when the Beatles broke up about ten or so years ago. We'd argued about who was the best one.

I swore it was Paul. Fat Freddie said John. Jimmy Lee, as dumb as the days are long, liked Ringo. We couldn't believe it back then, but Jimmy Lee had said, "If I'm lying, I'm dying," which for us was a blood oath. We was devastated when the Beatles broke up even though we mostly listened to country music. Merle, Willie, and Waylon. The Beatles did have a little Commie in them, but they was still the Beatles. It was almost like breaking up with a girlfriend you really liked. One that let you get to second base.

But that was nothing compared to Cosell's announcement of Lennon's shooting and death near the end of last week's game. The windbag, finally given something to sound pompous about, broke the news while New England lined up for a field goal. The three of us sat there and just stared at each other, unable to say a damned thing.

"Howard ain't never gonna announce something that awful ever again," Jimmy Lee said and we all nodded.

Wasn't often that Jimmy Lee said something smart, but he'd done it this time.

As if on cue, Cosell spoke up after another Rams first down.

"Ladies and gentlemen," he said in his trademark nasal voice. "We've been informed by ABC News of a stunning and singular event, some might even say preternatural. Science fiction come to life. An event which illustrates with painful clarity what a trivial, dare I say meaningless, endeavor football and yes, all of sports, truly are.

"Alien spacecraft larger than the very stadium where we are observing this game – and let me repeat, this is only a game – have arrived from somewhere in our vast universe, seeming to appear out of thin air, perhaps even another dimension in the Einsteinian sense."

I glanced at the freshly opened beer in my hand and squinted at the TV set. I set the Lone Star between my legs. I'd always been able to handle my liquor, but had I just heard what I thought I'd heard? I wiggled an index finger in one ear, then shook my head like a soaked dog spraying water everywhere. I thought I might have heard my brains rattling.

But Howard kept on. "These spaceships are now hovering over major cities across the globe. New York, Washington, D.C., Chicago, here in Los Angeles, London, Paris, Berlin, and reportedly Moscow, Peking, Rio de Janeiro, Bombay, and Baghdad." The screen cut away from the game to a shot of a vast mechanical clot of alien technology.

Jimmy Lee climbed out of the sofa and lumbered to the front door, not much more than pissing distance from where Fat Freddie and me remained seated. Jimmy Lee opened the door and looked out. "I don't see nothing." He shrugged, a confused look spreading across his bewhiskered face. He scratched himself. "It's kinda dark out, I guess. Maybe we'll see it in the morning."

"They didn't say one came to Dallas, you dumbass," Fat Freddie said. "Nearest one's probably that one in Los Angeles. You can't see there from here."

Jimmy Lee shrugged. "Could if it was big enough." But he sat back down, wriggling, I thought, to get away from the broken sofa springs.

Ferragamo completed another pass while Howard kept talking about the relative insignificance of football, using words like metaphysical, ethereal, mystical, and even Suey Generis, as if any of us was supposed to know who she was. He then said words that made all three of our jaws drop.

"We will be cancelling our usual halftime highlights to bring you Frank Reynolds in Washington, Max Robinson in Chicago, and Peter Jennings in London. They will update all of us on these transcendental developments that could affect every member of the human race."

"You gotta be shittin' me," Jimmy Lee said. "No highlights?"

Fat Freddie and I groaned. Howard hadn't been serious with that talk about football being insignificant. Anyone with half a brain could tell you that wasn't true. Football was wasn't just significant; it was *life*. Howard had just been saying that nonsense for the schoolteachers and librarians who were listening. Hadn't he?

"Why don't they do this news shit during commercials?" Jimmy Lee asked.

"It's gotta be some kinda joke," I said. "Like April Fool's in December."

Then the TV screen showed the three broadcasters. Nope, not a joke. One look at Dandy Don's ashen face answered that question.

Jimmy Lee looked at me. "What's transcendental?"

Forget *transcendental*, I thought. I was still stuck way back on *preternatural*.

EVEN AFTER THE know-it-alls ruined halftime, they kept interrupting the game in the third quarter and then said good-bye to Howard, Dandy Don, and what's-his-name at the start of the fourth. I suppose that shouldn't have made me so mad cause the 'Boys was getting their asses whipped, but it did. Rule Number One in Texas is don't mess with the Cowboys.

Jimmy Lee got up and went home, slamming the front door on the doublewide on his way out. Fat Freddie decided to stay for a bit longer after some guy named Carl Sagan came on the TV to talk about the aliens.

"I saw him on PBS," Fat Freddie blurted out, then covered his mouth, his eyes wide. He looked sheepishly at me.

"PBS?" I asked. "You watch PBS?"

"There's this series called *Cosmos* that caught my eye."

"PBS? What has this world come to?"

Fat Freddie shrugged. "It's got good music," he said defensively.

"You watch PB-freaking-S for the music?"

"I dunno," Freddie said, shifting in his seat, looking like he'd just farted in church. "It's about planets and stars and stuff."

"PBS," I said. "Well, I'll be." I looked at Fat Freddie, realizing I had an honest-to-goodness alien in my own house. Didn't need no TV for that. "Never thought I'd see the day."

"Hey, Clete, do me a favor, will ya?" Fat Freddie said, leaning close and talking like it was some kind of conspiracy and don't let nobody else hear nothing even though we was the only ones in the room. "Let's keep this between just you and me. Don't say nothing to Jimmy Lee."

I just stared at him.

"Didn't you never watch Sesame Street?" Fat Freddie asked, his eyes shifting like a criminal.

"That's different and you know it," I said, and he knew I was right.

I stared at him, feeling like Perry Mason in front of a guilty witness.

THE ALIENS DIDN'T DO a damned thing for the next week. They coulda done something while nothing but soaps was on or during the evening news, but no. They didn't do a goddamned thing. Just hovered over all the big cities – but not Dallas – like we was some kind of squirming bugs needing to be inspected underneath their microscopes.

For most of the week, that was about all you saw on the TV, all the smarty-pants experts telling us what to expect, most of them saying that these outer space critters must have come in peace else they'd have already blowed us up to kingdom come. That Sagan guy kept talking about *billions* of light years or something like that. All I know is it was *billions* and *billions*. I never could figure out what Fat Freddie saw in the guy.

Outgoing President Jimmy Carter didn't look like he knew whether to sneeze or take a shit. He kept saying that he would defer to "the President elect" as if he didn't know the guy's name was Ronald Reagan. Myself, I thought Reagan would nuke the fuckers like I'd been sure he was gonna do to the Iranians if they didn't turn over the hostages before he got hisself sworn in. But Reagan looked as scared shitless as Carter, saying over and over, "Let's wait to hear their message. We trust that they came in peace."

I really didn't much give a shit until some candy asses started talking about cancelling the NFL games that week-end. Then other candy asses said the NFL should cancel the season – the *season!* – and the colleges should cancel all the bowl games.

"Can you believe that?" I asked over the phone to Jimmy Lee, who'd become the first guy to call now that Fat Freddie had put hisself on the Suspicious list. "What the hell would we do on New Year's Day without the bowl games?"

"Damned if I know," Jimmy Lee said. "Probably get drunk."

"And what the hell do they think they're gonna accomplish by cancelling the NFL?" I asked, hearing panic in my voice. "Hell, it's Cowboys-Eagles this week. If we win, we're in the playoffs!"

"They can't cancel the games. The smarty-pants, girly men are just spittin' in the wind."

"If them aliens are gonna suck the life outta us, then let them fuckers try," I said. "Ain't no need for us to suck the life out all by ourselves. That's what cancelling the NFL season would do. That's what cancelling just this week would do. *Football is life!*"

"Preach it, Brother!" Jimmy Lee said.

We laughed just a little, but I was still steamed. "I don't much wanna watch TV at all now."

"I know what you mean," Jimmy Lee said. "If I have to see one of them news anchors one more time, I might have to kick in my TV set."

"That'd teach 'em," I said.

"Damned right," Jimmy Lee said.

I SUPPOSE we should be happy that the aliens didn't ruin the Cowboys game on Sunday, giving them a chance to beat the Eagles and get into the playoffs. Church was packed that morning and there was lots of hooting and hollering about sinnin' after Pastor Rick said that God was punishing us with them aliens giving us the evil eye because of our transgressions.

But I was sitting there mostly because Bobby Sue wouldn't go out with no atheists and if it meant I had a chance to get her in the back of my pickup, I'd go to church or let them aliens give me every evil eye they wanted to. But she didn't even want to look at me after service. She was too busy gabbing with her friends about the aliens. They was talking a mile a minute, mostly arguing over whether this meant the Rapture was about to happen.

Damn, I thought. Talk like that wasn't gonna make Bobby Sue cooperative.

So I went back home to worship in front of my TV set with Jimmy Lee and a fidgety Fat Freddie, who kept giving me nervous sidelong looks. Texas Stadium was full with Cowboys fans and they did lots of my kind of hooting and hollering, making noise about winnin', not sinnin'.

With all due respect to Bobby Sue's panties which I may never get to hold in my trembling fingertips, I'll take my Sundays afternoons with Coach Tom Landry over Sunday mornings with Pastor Rick until the cows come home.

So like I said, the aliens gave us one last weekend of pure joy before they ruined the last Monday Night Football game of the year. The San Diego Chargers was playing the Pittsburgh Steelers and it would have been a mighty fine game to end the regular season if we'd gotten a chance to watch it. Fat Freddie arrived with the three steaming pizza boxes and for once, Jimmy Lee brought the Lone Star. It shoulda been great.

Howard and Dandy Don were in fine form during the pregame, clad in their gold ABC sports jackets that made them look like preachers of the Gospel of the two-minute drill. Even Frank Gifford looked okay as none of them had that frozen, nervous look they'd left us with a week ago.

"If I may opine," Cosell said.

"You always do, Howard," Dandy Don said, wearing his characteristic shit-eating grin.

"Many have pontificated about the reason for the alien

spaceships over our great cities," Howard said. "They arrived during this very same broadcast a week ago and have yet to deign us with an explanation. Perhaps, as some have speculated, they are still rousing themselves from interstellar sleep. Perhaps, as others have feared, they are deciding on our fate. Or perhaps they already know that fate and are taunting us like the great Muhammad Ali during a title fight.

"Until they choose to make their appearance and unveil their intentions, I will ally myself with those who contend that these aliens have come to us with good will toward all men and women," Howard said. "They crossed the great interstellar space using technologies we can only hope to fathom in an attempt to commune with another sentient species.

"If, however, the aliens mean us unspeakable harm, they will see that the peoples of Earth will come together as never before. We will answer any threat unified, responding as one because, in fact, we are one. One human race of many nationalities, languages, colors, and creeds. But in the end, we are one. And we will emerge victorious.

"I speak not for the diplomats of Earth, of course, but solely as one humble commentator."

Cosell blinked rapidly and fell silent.

"Humble?" Dandy Don gave Howard another shit-eating grin. "Howard, did you really say that?"

"Danderoo," Cosell said, "We all must be humbled at least a little by knowing that in the impossible vastness of space, we are no longer alone."

The telecast broke for a commercial. We all looked at each other, already washing down our second and third slices of pizza with our second and third Lone Stars. With every new cigarette, the blue cloud of smoke grew thicker.

"If they're gonna talk about this shit all night long," Jimmy Lee said, "I'm going home right now and blow out my brains."

"You ain't a good enough shot to hit that small a target," Fat Freddie said, almost choking on his slice of pepperoni as he yucked it up over his brilliant wit.

We enjoyed good fortune for less than a full quarter. Terry Bradshaw and Dan Fouts threw passes to Lynn Swann and Kellen Winslow. Franco Harris and Chuck Muncie ran the ball. And Howard, Dandy Don, and Frank actually talked about football. Imagine that, football. It felt like honey on a sore throat.

Then the goddamned aliens made their appearance, not descending from their spaceships or anything, and not even waiting until halftime. They just took over the TV set.

"Greetings to all humans," a voice said in a warm, familiar Texas accent. As if it was one of us. The screen filled with a view of Planet Earth from outer space, looking all blue except for the swirling whites of clouds. I realized that the alien voice was not coming from the TV set, which had fallen silent, but from within my own head.

"We have observed your species for a long time," it said. "Recently, we determined that corrective action was neces-sary because as a species you have stagnated. We are now interceding so that you may progress to the next level."

"What if we like the level we're at now?" Jimmy Lee asked, a sliver of pizza cheese hanging off his beard like a bright yellow booger.

Fat Freddie and I shushed Jimmy Lee silent.

"Individually, you waste exorbitant amounts of time on things that are not productive to you achieving your full potential," the alien voice said. "Many of you spend every waking hour attempting to mate."

"Mate? What are they talking about?" Jimmy Lee said. "I don't take but two or three minutes."

"While the need to reproduce is fundamental," the alien continued, "your mechanisms are hopelessly inefficient. We will guide you to processes that will free your energies to be spent in a more fruitful way."

I never much cared for people telling me what to do, but this alien was talking my language. If he and his people could show me a quicker way to get in Bobby Sue's pants, I was all for it.

"A second problem of your people," the alien said, "is your addictions that destroy your bodies and fracture your emotions. We will provide 'upgrades' that will eliminate these self-destructive impulses. You will no longer crave heroin or cocaine...."

Me, Jimmy Lee, and Fat Freddie nodded our approval and began lighting new cigarettes.

The alien continued. "Whiskey and beer will no longer hold their grip on your souls. They will no longer kill your brain cells."

We looked at each other wide-eyed and quickly gulped down the rest of our beers.

"You will desire," the alien said, "only the amount of food that your body requires and you will prefer the healthiest alternatives."

Each of us dove at another slice of pizza.

"Tobacco products will become a thing of the past."

We simultaneously took in the deepest of drags.

"Finally," the alien said, its voice suddenly light and lively, "you will end your pointless pursuit of those things you call sports. Your energies and time will no longer be wasted on football, basketball, baseball, hockey, golf, and NASCAR. There will be no more World Cup soccer or the Olympics. All those silly games that you have thrown away so many hours on will be removed. It will be a shock at first, but eventually you will feel a burden lifted from your shoulders."

I realized my jaw had dropped wide open only when I saw Jimmy Lee and Fat Freddie in the same condition. Loose ash fell from the glowing tips of our unsmoked cigarettes.

I narrowed my eyes. "Who the hell do they think they are?" I roared. My fists clenched and I gritted my teeth.

"They're taking away everything that makes life worth living," Fat Freddie said.

"Yeah," Jimmy Lee said. "Fucking, food, and football."

THE ALIEN SIGNED OFF, promising a new and improved human race, one ready to achieve its full potential. The TV returned to the football game, which appeared to have taken a long timeout during the alien's broadcast.

Howard began to talk, but I wasn't listening. The time for action was now. I went to my tiny bedroom closet and on the shelf above where my Sunday suit hung, I retrieved my double-barreled shotgun. I grabbed ammo from the box on the shelf and loaded the shotgun.

"Clete," Fat Freddie said from the open bedroom doorway. My bed was unmade and the sheets smelled sour. "It ain't that bad. Don't do nothing stupid."

I walked past him and Jimmy Lee and kicked open the doublewide's front door. As I walked down the steps, I heard the two rustle along behind me. The air felt clean and cool. I walked until I stood beside my black pickup truck.

"What are you doing, Clete?" Fat Freddie asked.

I pointed my shotgun to the sky and imagined one of the alien spacecraft hovering above me. I aimed and fired, the kick almost blowing my shoulder off. The roar of the shotgun rang in my ears. I aimed again, this time more slowly, seeing in my mind's eye the spaceship's bulls-eye on its underbelly. I pulled the trigger.

I heard Fat Freddie and Jimmy Lee whisper.

"I'll get my gun," Jimmy Lee said. "I'll be right back.

"Me, too," Fat Freddie said.

Off in the distance, I heard a single report at first and then a second and a third and a fourth. They came from off to the South and then to the West and then in all directions.

It sounded like the Fourth of July.

And in a way, it was.

Them aliens might be pretty smart, I thought, but they were also pretty dumb. They didn't know us very well at all.

It was Day One of their rule and The Rebellion had already begun.

The history books will record that in Texas, you don't ever fuck with football.

WHO I AM

INTRODUCTION TO WHO I AM

I wrote "Who I Am" for a Young Adult anthology entitled *Wishes.* I knew I was gambling with a volatile topic, so I shouldn't have been surprised when that gamble initially blew up in my face. Even so, it still stings whenever it happens. (And to be honest, when you play riverboat gambler with one story after another and keep getting away with it, you begin to think you're invincible.)

At first, the gamble seemed to have paid off. One of the six professional editors discussing the story at that year's WMG Anthology workshop called it "an extremely important story," said it caught him on the first page and hooked him, and if he were editing that particular anthology—which he wasn't—it would be a strong buy. Since he knew me as the writer of the award-winning thriller story "Death in the Serengeti," he added that he was "shocked that the tough Serengeti guy wrote this story."

Wow! A great endorsement.

Then the actual editor of the *Wishes* anthology, the

person who would make the thumbs up or thumbs down decision, called it "a gender version of 'Flowers for Algernon.' "

I almost keeled over.

My earliest and most longed-for writing dream was to some day write a story so amazing, so breathtaking it would stand the test of time. It would be remembered long after I'm gone. Specifically, a story like Harlan Ellison's "Jeffty is Five" or Daniel Keyes's "Flowers for Algernon."

Those were my two creative mountains that towered high above all others.

And this editor had just put "Who I Am" in the same sentence with that spectacular, legendary story. I... could... not... believe... it.

My story!

And then...

She rejected it.

Again, I almost keeled over. How could that be?

The reasoning was that in an anthology filled with the equivalent of sweet candies and treats, "Who I Am" was a candied apple loaded with razor blades. It just didn't fit.

I was crushed.

I'd had many stories before that "just didn't fit," and that was okay. At least mostly okay. I was never happy about it. After all, I'm human (allegedly). You're never happy when one of your literary babies is rejected. But it's a risk I accept every time my story zigs while others zag.

Just not this time.

Not with my "gender version of 'Flowers for Algernon.' "

That was a gut punch.

Oh, I tried to put on a good face and say all the right things. After all, I was "the tough Serengeti guy."

But I was also the "gender version of 'Flowers for Algernon' " guy.

Argh! Mommas, don't let your babies grow up to be writers.

Fast forward two years to the next Anthology Workshop. Until the pandemic hit, I attended every one of these workshops except for one, when a little thing called open-heart surgery stopped me. Each year, I learned so much and *loved* the opportunity to write for professional anthologies. Inevitably, I'd write stories on topics and themes, and sometimes in genres, I never would have otherwise considered. Most of them sold somewhere if not for the intended anthology, and a large number now appear in these collections of mine.

A total win.

Every year, I'd receive with mounting excitement the assignments to write for the six theme-based anthologies, each with a one-week deadline. And every year, I'd write those six stories come hell or high water. Professional writers don't let obstacles stop them. I cared enough to make sure I wrote the best story I could and submitted it before the Sunday midnight Pacific Time deadline.

Except once.

I failed one time. It was for an anthology to be called *Face the Strange,* edited by the same Ron and Brigid Collins duo I mentioned back in the introduction to "The Soulmate Junkie and the Beating Heart." Somehow, that one time, I got myself so tangled up in the various ideas I pursued that I had no completed story at the deadline.

I was mortified. Not only was it a missed opportunity —I *devoured* these opportunities—but I had let down my respected friends, Ron and Brigid. I never want to let down any editor, friend or total stranger. I always want to deliver the best story possible. And to be sure, I'd also let myself down. But to bat 1.000 in completing stories on deadline year after year only to fail for the very first time when writing for two great friends? My embarrassment and self-loathing knew no bounds.

I expressed those emotions to Ron and Brigid over and over when we met at the workshop. I was so sorry. I'm a total idiot. I don't know what's wrong with me.

"Don't worry about it," Ron said with his characteristic warm smile, seconded by Brigid.

But I did worry about it when it came time for them to discuss the stories submitted for *Face the Strange* and announce which ones made the cut. They might have hated whatever I had come up with, but I had still failed them. I hadn't given them a chance to pick a story of mine. I was such a loser.

Eventually, their list of accepted stories became complete except for one "mystery story" of about three thousand words that might or might not be available.

"Dave Hendrickson," Ron said from the podium. "Is your story 'Who I Am' still available?"

I almost fell off my chair. I don't think I've ever been more astonished. Someone took a photo of me at that instant, obviously amused at my look of total shock, and I have since saved it under the filename gobsmacked.jpg.

I'm notoriously slow, more accurately *glacial*, at resubmitting stories after they get rejected. I also go first to the very top markets, some of which are ridiculously slow to respond. For example, I submitted "Who I Am" to *The New Yorker*, in some eyes the most elite of elite publications and also one that never bothers to respond unless you've hit the lottery of an acceptance. You have to figure out that your story has been rejected by virtue of the length of time you've been ignored.

So between my shooting for the uppermost (seemingly impossible) markets and being a total slug when it comes to resubmitting, yes, the story was available! Cue up the Hallelujah Chorus! I was beyond euphoric and so very grateful that Ron and Brigid had remembered "Who I Am" and showed such astounding support for it.

Simply amazing.

Face the Strange was originally to be part of the *Fiction River* line of anthologies, but the pandemic foiled that plan. As a result, Ron and Brigid published it under Ron's imprint, Skyfox Publishing. Yet another reason for gratitude on my part.

Thanks to Ron and Brigid from the bottom of my heart.

WHO I AM

I wish I were a woman.

I think those words—knowing they will consign me to the depths of Hell if my actions haven't already—as I stare at myself in the full-length mirror.

A freak.

My sister's bedroom is little more than an oversized closet, maybe ten feet by twelve, the closed door on my left, the neatly made bed behind me, the backs of my knees touching it. The thin mirror, barely two feet wide, squeezes into the corner by the door, Sarah's second-hand, dark wood dresser to the right of it. To my right, kitty-corner with the dresser, is Sarah's small pinewood desk, papers neatly stacked on the side and her well-worn, leather-covered Bible square in the middle, accusing me.

The room is uncomfortably chilly, as it will be all winter long to save on heating oil, but that isn't why my arms are wrapped around myself, holding myself tight.

I drop my hands to my side and look at myself in the mirror. Sandy blond hair, fair complexion, almost no visible body hair due to its light hue, and a slender build for an average-sized eighteen-year-old boy. But that's the only thing that's average or remotely normal about me. I only notice my hair and physique because it contrasts with everything else I stare at.

I am naked except for my sister's plain white brassiere and panties.

A freak.

I stare at the plainness of her lingerie, wishing it could be pink and frilly like the ones in the Victoria's Secret commercials that we have to turn away from when they come on the TV. Such things are of the Devil, and they would be even if Sarah were wearing them.

On me, they would be an abomination.

But I can't help myself. If only I were a woman, standing here like this would not sentence me to an eternity in Hell.

With my heart hammering and hands shaking, I take a pair of my sister's pantyhose from the top left dresser drawer, and slip them on. I stare at myself and wish there were more than just talcum powder atop the dresser, its faint smell filling the air. I wish there was a wig, lipstick, and mascara so I could look even more like the woman I surely was meant to be. But Sarah, sixteen years old, not yet a woman herself, owns no wig or lipstick. No mascara or any of those worldly enticements. No earrings or necklaces, her only jewelry a plain watch she must be wearing now.

She is the good preacher's kid. Virtuous, her heart whiter than the snow piled three feet high outside. People like to gossip about preacher's kids, hoping to knock us off our pedestals, but she gives them no ammunition.

If only they knew about me. I watch myself shiver in the mirror and taste bile in the back of my throat. They'd have a field day with me, weeping and wailing at the altar, appalled yet fascinated by my perversion, thanking the Good Lord they have been spared the humiliation of giving birth to a wretched freak like me.

But no one knows.

Everyone thinks I'm as saintly as my sister, prepared to go to Bible College next year, almost as saintly as my mother and my father, Rev. Jonathan Templeton, pastor at Calvary Baptist for over ten years. Hundreds of people flock from all about Boston's South Shore to hear him preach in one of two Sunday morning services, an evening service, and a midweek service on Wednesday nights.

He would, of course, be ruined if my sinful secret became public. Disgraced. Unfit for God's calling for having spawned a child of the Devil like me.

And yet I stand here, my own clothes in a clump on the threadbare light brown carpet, wishing I had breasts to fill out my sister's brassiere. It wouldn't take much. She's boyishly flat-chested, but I, of course, have nothing. I think of going downstairs to the kitchen to get a pair of oranges or apples to form my breasts. I need something to—

Downstairs, the front door opens and slams shut.

"David?"

My eyes widen. My father! What is he doing here? No one was supposed to be home for another two hours. My heart, pounding with excitement seconds before, now jackhammers with terror.

As silently as possible, I slide shut the drawer from which I'd taken Sarah's panty hose. I reach back to unhook her brassiere, the straps tight across my back and over my shoulders, but I fumble with the clasp, my usually nimble fingers trembling and numb with panic.

My father's footsteps thunder up the stairs. "Sarah? David?"

I freeze for only a second. Then I shove my clothes under the bed and fall to my knees to flatten myself against the tattered carpet.

Fearful that I will tear Sarah's pantyhose, but far, far, far more fearful of the footsteps coming down the hallway, I slide beneath her bed, barely fitting beneath the box spring. I bang my head twice as I push my clothes ahead of me, grabbing the lone black sock I almost left out in plain view as I inch my way to the wall against which the bed is set.

I close my eyes.

Dear Jesus, please help me. Please, please, please. I'll never do this again. I'll do whatever you want. I'll even be a missionary to Africa. Please, don't let him catch me like this. Please, please, please.

My father raps on the door to my bedroom, fifteen feet further up the hallway, its rear wall abutting the one holding Sarah's mirror, where seconds before I gloried in my abomination.

Please, please, please.

"David?" The hinges creak as he opens that door, then creak again as he closes it.

Please, please, please.

He knocks on the door to this bedroom. I hold my breath and try to calm the thunderous pounding of my heart. My mouth is dry. Though the air is hot and dusty, I shiver.

"Sarah?"

My nose twitches, irritated at the dust I've stirred up. *Please, God, no*, I pray as I fight back the sneeze that will end my life.

The door opens and my father steps inside. He knows I'm here. I'm sure of it. Either he heard me or God is pointing him to the abomination that is his own son.

This is my son in whom I am so very displeased.

But displeased isn't the start of it. Disgraced. Humiliated. Horrified.

A freak.

I think of the brassiere, panties, and pantyhose I am wearing and feel none of the satisfaction of moments ago. Only horror at what I have become.

I watch my father's freshly polished black shoes move across the carpet, step by agonizingly slow step. The right one squeaks ever so slightly. He is seconds from dropping to one knee and peering under the bed.

Seeing me for what I am.

Please, dear Jesus, I'll do anything. Anything!

My father clears his throat.

Please!

And he leaves the room.

I COWER under the bed for fifteen minutes that feel like fifteen hours or even fifteen days, holding my breath as I sneeze even though it feels as though I'm blasting my eardrums out. Finally, my father leaves the house, slamming the door behind him.

I feel different as I slide out from beneath the bed. I am so ashamed. Jesus may have died for my sins, but he surely didn't die for me dressing up in my sister's underwear.

I am pathetic. A freak and the worst of sinners. I don't deserve to live.

I refuse to look in the mirror. I'm still wearing the same lingerie I couldn't take my eyes off of such a short time ago, but the shame and terror still cover me like a shroud.

I will never, ever, ever do this again, I tell myself, even though this isn't the first time and I know it won't be the last. But the humiliation overwhelms me. I refuse to look at myself like this.

Until I cast a glimpse out of the corner of my eyes.

My jaw drops. My eyes widen.

I am a woman.

I STARE at my image in the mirror, frozen and uncomprehending. My sandy blond hair hasn't suddenly grown to girlish lengths. That much and facially, I am unchanged. But breasts have blossomed to life, filling Sarah's brassiere.

My brassiere.

And the bulge between my legs that had made a mockery of my wish no matter how hard I tried to ignore it is now gone.

I touch myself down there in wonder and then lift a hand to my modest-sized breasts. This is no optical illusion, no byproduct of a funhouse mirror. My torso has somehow reformed, its muscle and fat redistributed, to give me a feminine hourglass-like shape. My skin feels softer, my body hair even finer and less visible. My Adam's apple, never prominent before, has shrunk to almost nothing.

I am a woman.

Now what am I supposed to do?

I am both thrilled and terrified.

But... what... am... I... supposed... to... do?

AFTER A VERY LONG time spent staring into that mirror, seeing myself as I always thought I should be, I reluctantly take off Sarah's undergarments. Somehow, I have avoided tearing her panty hose, and after folding her lingerie and putting everything back in the same dresser drawer and in the exact same position from which I took it – top left for the panty hose and top right for the bra and panties, panties toward the rear and bras up front – I stare in the mirror at my naked body and wonder at the miracle.

This isn't God's work. This is no answered prayer. I can't pretend that it is. I am still an abomination in His eyes.

But is this the work of Satan? I've made no deal with the Devil. All I begged for—and that was from the Lord was that I be left undiscovered.

And then I remember.

I wish I were a woman.

I stare into the mirror at the fulfillment of that wish. And I ask myself again, *what do I do now?*

BACK IN MY OWN BEDROOM, laid out just like Sarah's except that my mirror is a small rectangular one hung over the dresser, I pull on my pajamas and crawl beneath the covers. When my parents return home, I'll have to feign sickness, at least until I figure out what to do next. In the meantime, though, I explore my new body, the one I have secretly begged so long for.

This is who I am. I am a woman. I am blissfully, gloriously, and abundantly a woman. Released from the shackles of my male body.

I'm deliriously, out-of-my mind happy.

And at the same time, utterly terrified. What will my parents say? What will they do with me? And what about all my friends at school and at church?

This is not a secret I can keep. They'll treat me like the freak I always thought I was, always knew I was. They'll shun me. Ridicule me. Persecute me. Beat me. Or worse.

And I'll deserve it because surely I am the spawn of Satan.

Or am I?

⸺

THE NEXT DAY, Sunday, my father answers that question in no uncertain terms in his sermon.

I wake up exhausted, having kept myself awake most of the night, amazed and fascinated by my authentic femininity, and fearful that I would wake and find it stolen from me, all of it just a dream. I do feel somehow slightly less a woman this morning, my already small breasts a little bit tinier, the curve of my hips less pronounced. It may all be in my head, I suspect, perhaps a byproduct of my exhaustion. But I can hardly go into Sarah's room and examine myself closely to be sure. Perhaps whoever or whatever has changed my body is showing deference to where I'll spend most of the day, in church, singing hymns and listening to my father preach.

I've concealed my new identity, finding an old T-shirt two sizes too small and pulling it on, snug against my breasts, and then adding my usual Sunday-best white, button-up shirt, dark blue tie, and black suit. Sitting in the hard wooden pew between my mother and Sarah, both of them in their Sunday-best dresses, I conclude that no one could possibly detect my secret.

No one, that is, but Jesus.

My father has chosen his sermon as if he looked under that bed and saw what I was or what I have become. He's preaching to the congregation of two hundred fifty or so, a hellfire-and-brimstone sermon about God punishing the wickedness of Sodom and Gomorrah.

"We have become a wicked nation that has lost its spiritual compass," he preaches, looking down on the congregation from the elevated stage, standing behind the dark wood pulpit. Many respond with an amen. "It has become fashionable to accept that which God says must be condemned as sin, especially in the area of homosexuality and other deviant lifestyles."

He looks at me and my heart freezes. My palms become clammy. I can guess what he is about to say. *I came home yesterday to find my own dear boy dressed in his sister's underwear. My boy, already accepted to Bible College. And even worse, he is now a woman! David, my son, you can conceal what you have become from others, but you cannot hide from the eyes of God! Confess your sins and come back to Jesus! Confess your sins or burn in Hell for all eternity!*

But he says none of that.

Instead, his eyes move right on past me, and he continues, "The secular humanists would have us believe it is just an *alternative lifestyle,* no different than deciding whether to order a steak or chicken at a restaurant, no more important than becoming a fan of one sports team versus another." My father takes his leather-bound Bible off the pulpit and waves it. "But that's not what my Bible says. My Bible says it is a stench in the nostrils of the Lord."

A chorus of amens answers him, but I tune him out. Instead, I think of how I should be wearing Sarah's light blue dress, demurely long-sleeved and its hem well below the knee, and beneath it, her underwear, instead of this loathsome man's suit and underwear. I should have my legs crossed in a womanly fashion instead of sitting here masquerading as a young man. Pretending to be what I am not. I shouldn't have to conceal my breasts in a T-shirt as tight as a corset from bygone days.

I am a woman.

BUT NOT FOR LONG.

I had thought on Sunday that my decreased femininity might have all been in my head, a figment of my imagination. But it was not.

This morning, Monday, my small breasts have shrunken to a size barely more than that of a boy's. And though I refuse to look at it, I can tell there is a penis growing back between my legs. I'd be a spectacle to be sure if I had to take a shower in gym class, but I only have gym on Wednesdays and Fridays. At this rate, I'll be sadly "normal" in another day.

Normal.

The idea makes me snort in derision. It also makes me want to cry. For I have never been normal.

Until these blissful three days of womanhood, I was a freak. Anything but normal.

And that is what I will become again.

I STAY AWAKE in bed as long as I can, knowing it is my last night as a woman. I want to prolong the experience of being in a body that is who I am even if it is rapidly slipping away.

But in the darkness of my bedroom, I finally weaken, my eyes heavy, and I slip off to sleep. When the shrill ringing of the alarm on my desk awakens me to a new day, I am no longer who I have been. I am no longer a woman. Not even a hint remains of what I was these past three days.

When I was allowed to be who I really am.

I had to conceal it from the rest of the world, but for three magical, wonderful, terrifying days, I wasn't a freak.

I was me.

What changed me? How was I transformed? What answered my wish?

I wish I were a woman.

It wasn't an answered prayer from the Lord I've tried to

serve. Much as I'd love to convince myself otherwise, I know better. And I made no request of the Dark Lord. If I am the child of Satan, I am an involuntary one.

Was my transformation, temporary as it was, triggered by some yet-to-be-understood biological reaction to the sheer terror I felt at being caught in Sarah's lingerie? If that's all it takes, then I suppose it won't be long before I take that chance again.

I'll come as close as I possibly can to being discovered. I'll become a fan of that terror even as it transforms me. I'll revisit it time and time again until inevitably I am caught.

I long already for a return of that body. My body. Perhaps it will never come back to me in that magical way. My only solution will be the treatments and surgeries offered by doctors. With that, will come the scorn and abandonment of those I love the most. For there is no secret with a change such as that.

I have much to consider. But no matter what befalls me, these past three magical, mysterious days have been a gift. I have been given the greatest of all gifts.

I know now who I am.

I am not a freak.

I am me.

HUSKIE AND PUNKIN'

INTRODUCTION TO HUSKIE AND PUNKIN'

I wrote this story for WMG Publishing's *Halloween Spectacular*, a spinoff from its wonderfully innovative *Holiday Spectacular*, an advent calendar of fiction that sends subscribers a short story each day from Thanksgiving to New Year's. The daily dose of these Halloween-themed stories would similarly span nine autumnal days surrounding that most unique of holidays.

Even before I sat down to write, the image came to me of... well... I hate spoilers, so let's just say that the image came to me of Huskie. You'll meet him shortly and if I did my job well, you'll become as entranced with him as I did. Huskie and I had a great time together with this story, and the same can be said for Punkin'.

Great fun.

The *Halloween Spectacular* editor, Mark Leslie, shared my enthusiasm for the story. He didn't just buy it, he said, "I *love* this story. I have to have it for the anthology."

Them's what we writers call sweet words indeed.

HUSKIE AND PUNKIN'

*L*ifeless, his essence ripped from him over a moon ago, Huskie awoke.

Gotta find my Punkin'.

A chill breeze whipped through the endless rows of tattered cornstalks that stretched as far as the eye could see. Many moons ago, when the sun rose high and bright in the sky and the stalks were all still green and vibrant and still held an ear or two of juicy, sweet essence, they had whispered among themselves of this hallowed day.

The Day of Days.

The day when they would all awake from the loss of their essence and even though they had been rendered dry, brittle, brown shells of themselves, they would be rooted in one place no longer. They would triumphantly walk and talk like the humans that passed through their endless rows. They would dance, they would frolic, and they would sing songs of their abundant life.

It could all be a lie, Huskie had often thought, though

never whispered. A wonderful lie of hope, one invented to keep them content and rooted in their place even as their looming fate hung over them all. A fate that they would not only be shorn of their essence, as had already come to pass, but they would also surely burn.

If not for the Day of Days, they would burn to nothing but ash. Fertile ash, but nothing more.

Flames would lick at the dry leaves wrapped around their stalks, then shoot up the stalks while burning inward, consuming them slowly as they screamed their death song.

Huskie shuddered. The tattered tip of a brown, brittle leaf of his broke off and wafted away in the chill breeze. The smell of decay rose from the ground.

The Day of Days *had* to be true. His fate *had* to be better than consuming flames.

And he had awoken today, hadn't he? But so much more had been promised in the whispers in the fields. He remained rooted exactly where he had always been rooted, surrounded by the same stalks that had surrounded him his entire life.

Some Day of Days this was!

Gotta find my Punkin'.

Huskie wasn't sure where that thought came from. He'd never heard it whispered in the fields by the others. Huskie wasn't even sure what it meant. Who or what was Punkin'? Where was she? And why was he convinced that Punkin' was a she and not a he? Or just an it?

Gotta find my Punkin'.

Huskie tugged at one side of his roots and then the other, trying to break free of the hard earth while maintaining enough balance to remain upright.

No luck.

He tried again. And then again. Tugging wasn't working. And yet if he did anything more, he would surely topple to the ground and never stand tall again.

Gotta find my Punkin'.

Huskie did more than tug. He pulled and pulled, first one side and then the other.

And then Huskie strained with all his might. *Strained.*

A chunk of earth at the base of his stalk crumbled apart. And then another. A beetle, apparently awoken from its own hibernation, scuttled from the crumbled earth in one confused direction and then another.

Huskie strained again with all his might, and...

... the right side of his roots pulled free!

Suddenly, Huskie felt himself tilting wildly to the left, almost toppling over. He strained with his remaining embedded roots of the left to push himself back upright.

Slowly, slowly, he made it.

Standing as tall as he could manage now that he was a shell of himself, Huskie saw with dismay that he had shed more brown, dry leaves in the struggle. They coated the ground.

He couldn't do this, he thought. The best he could hope for was to pull free of the ground and then fall flat on his side. He might be trying a lot harder than all the stalks around him, who seemed to be doing nothing, but he'd wind up worse off than they would. By the end of this not-so-hallowed day, they would still at least be alive.

He'd be lying on his side, roots pulled free, dying a quicker death than all those around him who at least knew what they were. They were cornstalks, as was he, and cornstalks don't walk.

Even on the Day of Days.

Gotta find my Punkin'.

Who was Punkin'? Huskie had to find out. And if he died trying, that was better than not trying at all, wasn't it? Huskie whispered that thought aloud to the other stalks—*better to die trying than not try at all*—so that perhaps that insight might inspire someone, anyone, or it might even survive him in the collective mind.

He sensed, though, that no one was listening. They might even be mocking his arrogance.

Well, so be it. He wouldn't be like all the others who had whispered so lovingly of this coming day, but now that it had arrived, cowered instead in abject fear.

Not him.

Gotta find my Punkin'.

Huskie strained at the front part of his left-side, still-embedded roots, and slowly they tore free, too. He almost toppled over backwards, but righted himself.

And then he tore free half of the remaining embedded roots, and then half of the remaining half, again and again, until finally...

... he was free!

Huskie stood atop his tangled roots, wriggling them like he'd seen a humans do once when it was barefoot.

A light breeze gusted and almost toppled Huskie. He barely steadied himself on his wriggling roots.

And then, lurching as if he were a drunken human, he stepped out into the empty row, the ground uneven beneath his wriggling roots, and pointed himself in the direction of the still rising sun, the direction his instincts had suggested.

With his wriggling roots acting like the legs of caterpillars that had climbed up his stalk so many times, Huskie moved with increasing steadiness down the row. He sensed the whispers of his cowardly brothers on all sides, the gasps of surprise and even shock.

Go back before it's too late. It's only one day. Then what? It isn't worth the risk.

But Huskie had never felt more alive.

Gotta find my Punkin'.

SET back twenty yards from the lightly used state highway, Thompson's Farm Stand offered the best fruits and vegetables in the area. In past months, customers had streamed from the local towns to purchase their tomatoes, sweet corn, lettuce, spinach, kale, strawberries, cucumbers, and carrots. But on this day, Halloween, they were standing at the front counter beneath the red-and-white-striped canopy asking for pumpkins.

Perched on the counter on the far left side was a basketball-sized jack-o'-lantern, its teeth sharp and garish and its candle burning brightly. Beside it was the most oddly shaped pumpkin, thin and angular in the shape of the letter I instead of the letter O, and covered with green blotches and wart-like bumps.

A conversation piece. The ugliest pumpkin in America. An amusement for the customers.

Punkin'.

Punkin' had never been more terrified in her life. She'd watched the pumpkin beside her get cruelly carved out, its essence spilled into a bag, and eyes, nose, and teeth carved into its face before a fire was lighted on a stick plunged within it.

A jack-o'-lantern. Barbarism.

Punkin' was mere inches away from it. She could even feel the heat of its flame.

She would choose any fate to avoid being the next one of its kind. She shuddered at the thought of her essence being carved out of her, every last bit scraped out, and then a burning stick planted inside.

This height also scared her. She'd spent her whole life on the ground. But it didn't scare her half as much as the carved-out fire beside her.

Huskie? Are you out there?

She didn't know who or what Huskie was, but the thought sprung from deep within her nonetheless.

Punkin' began to rock herself back and forth. Back and forth. Back and forth. With any luck, she'd topple from the counter and land on the hard ground below. She doubted that she could survive the fall. Most likely, she would splatter all her seeds on the ground.

But maybe, just maybe, she could harden herself as she fell and survive it, and on this Day of Days, roll away from her captors and be free.

And if not? What if her guts were to be splattered on the ground? Better that than be carved out while still alive, and have a burning stick plunged into your soul.

HUSKIE SEARCHED the fields without knowing what he was searching for, but sure he'd recognize Punkin' when he saw her. His faith waivered as he scanned one field after another, almost all of them barren or at least as barren as the cornfields had been. Still, he believed.

Gotta find my Punkin'.

He didn't find her until he made his way toward the road that passed by the farm. He had been avoiding the road. It scared him. He hated its harsh smell and that of the tractor-like things (only faster, much faster). When the largest of those things passed noisily by, Huskie had to pin himself against a tree or a fence to keep from being knocked down by the resulting wind.

Up close to the road, hiding behind an apple tree, Huskie looked upon a thing the humans called a farmstand. Made of painted white wood, it stood barely as tall as he was and as wide as the height of three corn stalks laid end-to-end. A young human with hair of straw stood in the opening of the stand and took paper from another human and in return gave it three plump, orange pumpkins. Huskie watched in fascination as the human took its pumpkins and carried them to its tractor-like thing and drove away.

And then Huskie saw her.

Punkin'.

She sat atop the counter where the humans had exchanged paper for the three plump pumpkins, but Punkin' could not have looked any differently than those others of her kind. Thin and angular where they were plump. Covered with blotches of green and wart-like bumps where they were smooth and orange.

Punkin' was not alone. Immediately to her left was a pumpkin that had once been perfectly formed, but one whose innards had been carved out, as had been holes to resemble a human's eyes, nose, and hideous teeth. Inside it, a flame burned on some kind of stick, the flame visible through the holes.

Huskie shuddered, as he always did at the very thought of fire, but also at the plight of Punkin', trapped beside this flaming thing of her kind, a fellow Huskie instinctively thought of as Jack O'Something. Jack O'Light. Or something like that.

Beside that flaming monstrosity, Punkin' rocked back and forth, and side to side, clearly attempting to get away from it.

Huskie told himself that was what he was here for.

Gotta find my Punkin'.

He had found her. Now, he had to somehow help her. Help her escape this flaming Jack-thing, and perhaps help her escape the farmstand itself before some other human came to claim her.

On his wriggling roots, Huskie moved out from the apple tree and crept toward Punkin'. He reached the side of the farmstand, and peered around its corner. The young human with hair of straw, however, stood at the opening. Huskie knew deep within himself, without knowing how he knew it, that no good would come of a human spotting him like this.

Fire.

It would probably come to fire. Perhaps feeding him to the burning Jack thing beside Punkin'.

Fire, the worst of Huskie's fears. Especially now that he was dry and brittle. Could he even make his way to Punkin' and come so close to the burning Jack thing? It would consume him in no time.

But Huskie had to help Punkin'.

With as hard a thwack of his upper stalk as Huskie could manage without breaking himself into two or toppling over, he hit the side of the stand to draw the human away from the opening. Then he dashed as fast as his wriggling roots could take him to Punkin'.

Even as his fears screamed about the dangers of the flaming Jack thing so very, very close—so close he swore he could *smell* the flame—Huskie opened to Punkin' the leaves that had once held his essence, beckoning Punkin' like a human with open arms.

THE DRIED-OUT CORNSTALK APPEARED BEFORE PUNKIN' and held out for her a cluster of brittle-looking, brown leaves.

Huskie?

Yes, somehow she knew this was Huskie. But what were these tattered leaves of his that he was holding out to her? Tiny as she was—and she'd heard all the disparaging comments from her kind back in the patch and then from the humans at the stand about how tiny could be cute, but she was far too misshapen and discolored for that—there was no way that this corn stalk's brittle leaves could support her. It would snap right off.

And if the leaves didn't break off, her weight might topple him over. He hadn't looked very steady as he had shambled over with all those roots of his wiggling away.

Huskie clearly hadn't thought this out very well. Or perhaps he simply wasn't very smart. She'd have to improvise a better plan, and do so before the human saw what they were doing.

Quickly, she rocked back, away from Huskie.

He hesitated for just an instant—Punkin' thought she heard a panicked gasp—and then he leaned forward to her.

Punkin' rolled on top of the extended cluster of leaves, pinning Huskie down, and took her chance. It might not be much less dangerous than just taking the plunge off the counter—it was hardly different at all—but it was the best shot she had. It was, she thought, why this Huskie had come to her.

Punkin' rolled along the pinned-down leaves, her wart-like, uneven surface causing her to wobble unsteadily, and then she bounced onto the corn stalk that was bent ever so slightly toward the counter and—

—she plummeted down the stalk's precipitous, almost cliff-like surface.

Downward she rolled and bounced with dizzying speed, using her warts to slow herself ever so slightly and skid along the cornstalk's dry surface, but faster and faster she dropped.

She would end splattered on the brown, dirt ground below that was racing up to meet her. She was sure of it. Splat!

Huskieeeeee!

Punkin' braced for the impact and the end of her days,

her skidding not slowing her down nearly enough. Her seeds would be splattered and then swept away. Not worth planting, as the humans had said, because who would want more of her?

And then—

Huskie suddenly, somehow curved the base of his stalk, turning it into a ramp, converting her blinding speed from the vertical to the horizontal.

Punkin' shot sideways to the ground—*weeee!* she squealed with petrified glee as she flew through the air—not touching down until she was many cornstalk lengths from the stand.

She bounced hard on the ground, its grit tearing away some of her bumps and skin, then rolled on and on until finally she came to a rest.

Full of jubilation, she looked back to Huskie at the stand.

And screamed.

Huskie lay on the ground. Tufts of smoke rose into the air.

Punkin' rocked back and forth, then began to roll back to Huskie.

She rolled as fast as she could, bumping along the hard dirt ground, sure she wouldn't get there fast enough.

FIRE! Fire! Fire! Fire!

Huskie screamed the word—the worst word he knew—in utter panic as he toppled to the ground.

If he could run, he would run. If he could hide, he

would hide. Anything to get away from the flames, even though there was no escaping them.

Somehow, in all his bending and twisting gyrations to get Punkin' down safely, the tip of his extended leaves had brushed along the inside of the Jack-thing and touched the flame. Dry as a drought, it had ignited.

Staggering unsuccessfully to right himself after the gyrations, Huskie had crashed to the ground. He had extended the flaming leaves as far as he could from the rest of his body, but there was no detaching them. The flames would lick their way toward his main stalk and then slowly and gruesomely consume all of him.

His Day of Days would end in a fiery death after all.

Huskie thrashed side to side, slapping the flaming leaves —extended as far from the main stalk as he could get them —against the ground. It seemed to slow the burn, but didn't put it out. After a moment of smoky sparks, the flame shot up again.

Again, he slapped the leaves down and they smoked and sparked, but before they could ignite the final flame that would reach the stalk itself—

Punkin' rolled over the flickering leaves.

She skidded to a stop and then rolled back over them again.

Back and forth. Back and forth. Crushing the flame.

Until it was, for certain, out.

Thank you, thank you, thank you shouted Huskie from the depths of his being.

He had been rescued!

Except... he slowly realized that he hadn't been spared after all. No, he wouldn't suffer a fiery death, or at least he wouldn't until a human came to retrieve him, but he had no way to get back upright. Now that he was down, there was no getting back up again.

That had been the danger all along. That had been the warning whispered by all the other cornstalks in the field. Cornstalks were not meant to walk. This freedom was great and exhilarating while it lasted, but it wouldn't last. Couldn't last. He had defied the odds to have lasted as long as he had.

This was how his Day of Days would end, with him sprawled on the ground until a human came to dispose of him.

Thank you, he said to Punkin', who had rolled up to the top of his stalk and seemed to be radiating happiness despite the scars above her green-splotched, wart-ridden skin. *But I can't get up.*

Push up with one of the other leaves, she replied. *One that has a half-formed ear.*

The human had harvested Huskie's two primary ears, his essence, but two half-formed ears with their own kernels remained. He pushed up on those ears with all his might, but could get the top of his stalk only a few inches off the ground.

Worthless, Huskie thought.

Punkin', however, had other ideas.

She rolled into the several-inch gap between the tip of the stalk and the ground, and began to rock back and forth. Slowly, she began to roll toward the base of the stalk, lifting the tip first one inch, then two, and then three and four.

Whoa! Huskie thought, stunned at the brilliant idea. It couldn't possible get him fully erect, could it? Huskie shot out his leaves, like a human's arms, to steady himself as Punkin' slowly levered him higher off the ground.

When instead of rising higher he began to slide in the direction of Punkin's pressure, she spoke with what he thought might be a tone of annoyance.

Will you dig in? Please?

Huskie's roots couldn't penetrate the hard dirt surface very well, but when they found a barely submerged, foot-long rock, they latched on.

He hung on for dear life.

Slowly, Punkin' levered him higher. One foot off the ground. Two feet.

Huskie teetered for a moment, close to toppling off to the left, but he leaned hard to the other side and Punkin' moved him upward.

Higher and higher until he was almost upright with Punkin' near his base.

Huskie leaned back and Punkin' gave one last thrust.

Upright! He was upright!

Huskie staggered for a moment, almost continuing to lean back for too long, but stopping just in time, balancing with his two leaves filled half-formed ears. He released his pincer-tight grip on the rock, and stood euphorically erect.

Yes! they cried in unison.

You did it! Huskie cried, filled with gratitude. *You did it! That was amazing!*

Not until then did they spot the young human from inside the farmstand, her long hair the color of straw, clinging to the far corner of the stand, leaning heavily on it, her eyes wide open, her mouth agape.

"Mom! Come quick!" she yelled. "*Moooom!*"

Together, Huskie and Punkin' rolled and scuttled their way back through the cornfields and out past the edge of the farm. They encountered a dog that threatened to tear Huskie to shreds until Punkin' rolled in and acted like a ball, distracting it, rolling back and forth, back and forth, until finally it became bored and ran off.

They hid from humans. They ignored the whispers in the cornfields.

With great difficulty, Huskie and Punkin' scaled hills that felt like mountains and crossed creeks that felt like oceans. They explored life beyond the farm for the first time, and felt a feeling of freedom and friendship they had never before known.

They never wanted it to end.

But the Day of Days is but one day, as the whisperers had cautioned, and as midnight beckoned, Punkin' and Huskie found themselves standing on the banks of a small creek. The moon had risen high in the clear sky, visible through the tangle of overhead branches. Owls hooted.

Huskie wrapped his lower leaves around Punkin'. She leaned into the embrace.

What comes next? Punkin' asked.

I'm not sure, Huskie said.

Will we remember each other? Even just tomorrow?

I hope so.

For a time, the forest fell silent. Even the owls.

And then Punkin' spoke the last words before midnight struck.

On the next Day of Days, I hope our offspring have a day as wonderful as this.

MANY MOONS PASSED until on that hallowed day...

LIFELESS, his essence ripped from him over a moon ago, Huskie awoke.

Gotta find my Punkin'.

Thank you for your interest in my books.

D H H

NEWSLETTER

Be the first to know!

If you love my writing, my newsletter is a great way to keep up with new releases, special promotions, and other content that's only available to my newsletter subscribers.

What are you waiting for?

Sign up at www.hendricksonwriter.com/newsletter-free-story/ today!

Cape Cod Chips, Wiener Dogs, and Swiping Left: Stories of Sweet Romance (forthcoming)

The Soulmate Junkie and Other Stories of Fantasy & Science Fiction (forthcoming)

Crime From Another Time: Stories of Mystery and Suspense (forthcoming)

Crime Fantastique: Stories of Mystery and Suspense (forthcoming)

Crime, Up Close and Personal: Stories of Mystery and Suspense (forthcoming)

Nonfiction

How to Get Your Book Into Schools and Double Your Income With Volume Sales

Travis Roy: Quadriplegia and a Life of Purpose

Hendu's Story: From Dream to Reality

ACKNOWLEDGMENTS

To Dean Wesley Smith, Ron and Brigid Collins, Mark Leslie, and Leah Cutter, the editors who believed in these stories.

To Annie Reed, the editor and cover designer of this collection, whose expertise I can always rely on.

To my readers, whose enthusiasm helps keep me going.

To all my family and friends, who support me during the valleys and celebrate with me on the mountaintops.

And above all, to Brenda, The Best Wife Ever™, for always being there and filling life's journey with such joy.

ABOUT THE AUTHOR

David H. Hendrickson's first novel, *Cracking the Ice*, was praised by *Booklist* as "a gripping account of a courageous young man rising above evil." He has since published seven additional novels, including *Offside*, which has been adopted for high school student required reading.

His short fiction has appeared in *Best American Mystery Stories 2018*, *Ellery Queen's Mystery Magazine*, *Thrill Ride - the Magazine*, *Heart's Kiss*, almost every issue of *Pulphouse Fiction Magazine* and *Mystery, Crime, and Mayhem*, as well as numerous anthologies, including over a half dozen issues of *Fiction River*. He is a multi-finalist for the Derringer Award, and his story "Death in the Serengeti" was honored with the 2018 Derringer Award for Best Long Story.

He has published six short story collections with five more forthcoming. Currently available: *Shimmers and Laughs: Eight Wildly Hilarious Tales*; *Death in the Serengeti and Other Stories: Ten Tales of Crime*; *The Boy in the Boxers and Other Stories of Sweet Romance*; *Hell of a Band: Twelve Fantasy Stories*; *Fighting the Dying Light: Stories of Aging*; and *Cape Cod Chips, Wiener Dogs, and Swiping Left: Stories of Sweet Romance*.

Hendrickson has published over fifteen hundred works of nonfiction, most notably his first book for writers, *How* to Get Your Book into Schools and Double Your Income with Volume Sales, and also *Travis Roy: Quadriplegia and a Life of Purpose* and *Hendu's Story: From Dream to Reality*. He has been honored with the Joe Concannon Hockey East Media Award and the Murray Kramer Scarlet Quill Award.

Visit him online at www.hendricksonwriter.com.